THE DATING DARE

A.R. PERRY

Legendary Books

The Dating Dare

A.R. Perry

ONE
Lily

I'm not like other girls who read "teen-trash"

"REMIND me why we're going to this party again?"

Madison laughed from my bed and flipped another page in whatever teen-trash magazine she brought over. Nothing like celebrity gossip and how to get the guy articles to expand intellect. Then again, she never poked fun at me when she caught me reading a romance book. Even if the cover featured an all-muscle dude. Which is precisely why I kept my lips sealed when she pulled it out. We made a pact long ago that we were only allowed to call each other out on crap when it was serious. And her infatuation bordering on obsession with the Hemsworth brothers and the newest lipstick trends didn't fall into that category.

"You know why. We're celebrating the end of the year, the beginning of an amazing summer, and the fact that you and I are *officially* seniors." Her feet kicked her butt as she let out a squeal.

I scowled at my clothes or maybe at the simplicity of her answer. Of course, she saw the party that way. I, on the other hand, saw it as a loud mass of bodies crowded together into a tiny space. Nothing but a group of kids hoping to get into trouble and each other's pants. Especially since Hunter, the emperor of rule breaking, was throwing it. No doubt with his best friend, King Douche-McGouche right

OK

by his side. No way we wouldn't be breaking some kind of fire marshal code. Or a plethora of other laws. Which was not something I felt comfortable with.

"All anyone ever does is get wasted," I grumbled as I pulled out a black dress that I was certain I wore to my great aunt's funeral. When I was eleven. A donation to Goodwill would need to go on the summer to-do list.

"Yes, but you're so good at being designated driver," she called, in the sweetest singsong voice she could muster before I heard her feet hit the hardwood. "Now would you *please* pick something."

"All I have is school clothes."

"What's wrong with your school clothes?"

I gave a pointed look at her outfit before spinning around to thumb through the same articles of clothing I'd already passed over three times. Madison looked amazing per usual. Her mothers never capped her spending and never approved what she bought beforehand. Total opposite of helicopter parents.

Her chosen party outfit—which I made her wait to change into until my mother left—was a risqué combination of a white, frilly, crop top that was one sneeze away from showing underboob and a denim miniskirt she thought appropriate to pair with black, thigh-high, leather boots. If I tried to leave the house looking like that, my mother would have a heart attack, then come back to haunt me just to guilt me.

Thus the whole changing after my mother left.

"You look beautiful in everything you wear."

I snorted, pulling out an emerald-green, lacy, tank top. It would have to do.

"Seriously." Madison reached into my closet and grabbed a pair of dark-wash skinny jeans. She tossed them

immediatly no.

to me and leaned against the doorframe. "I have to try harder because I inherited my mother's short gene and my sperm donor's buck teeth. At least, I'm assuming I got that from him. I've never seen a picture of my mom with braces." She waved away her own rambling. "Me, on the other hand... 'Member how much I was teased? Now that I fixed the teeth, I gotta make sure I leave a better lasting impression."

I chuckled as I slipped on the jeans, doing a little shimmy to get them over my butt. Speaking of things that were inherited from parents... "That was how many years ago? You got your braces off before you even started high school."

So dramatic.

"Need I remind you we still go to school with kids that *do* remember? Like that water god that lives next door." Oh Geez

I wrinkled my nose at the mention of Parker. He had been my neighbor since we were in diapers, and a pain in my ass for the past four years. His recurring attempts to torment me and his perpetual man-whoring ways— including dating several of the girls that ran in our circle— pretty much put a nail in the coffin that would have been our friendship. Not to be judgy, mind you. I just figured if he hated me so much, he would steer clear of people I sat with at lunch and spent weekends with. Seeing him tongue-screw a girl's ear in the cafeteria was enough to make me almost lose my lunch. Perhaps my utter look of disgust is what got him off. Just another way to torture me. Though in truth, it had gotten to the point where breathing was enough to set me off.

Like a fly buzzing around that I just couldn't catch.

A wool sweater on a summer day.

I could go on and on. The point was, he annoyed me

beyond words, and the thought of my best friend hooking up with him made me want to puke then hold an exorcism to purge her from the almost demonic allure Parker possessed.

"Please don't talk about him like that, I'm trying really hard to keep dinner down as it is." I plopped down in my computer chair with a dramatic gag and ran a brush through my hair.

"Oh, come on. Yes, he's like king of douche town, but you have to admit he's hot."

It would never be something I would admit out loud. Never, ever. He was one of those people who ruined their good looks the second they spoke, and their inner self showed how ugly they actually were. But in truth, I was grateful for his inability to keep any of his thoughts inside his head. If he ever shut up for more than a few seconds, I would have to admit that he leaned more toward the side of panty-dropping model than he did soul-sucking demon spawn. That would be terrible for my ego. Thankfully for me, that day would never come.

"You need some makeup. And lucky for you..." Madison picked her backpack up from the floor and rummaged around until she came out with a blue-paisley makeup bag.

"Aren't I being tortured enough with you dragging me to this party?"

"Would you shut up already and admit it's going to be fun? Hunter's parents are out of town and the whole class, plus some recently graduated seniors, are going to be there. You know what that means? College boys. And I haven't dated one of those yet."

I laughed and flinched away as Madison tried to attack me with black eyeliner. Madison had a list of boys she intended to date before graduating. And by 'date', she meant hook up with. Chalk it up to being ignored for the first part of puberty, but the girl was on a roll. She'd already dated a boy from pretty much every sports team our school had. Then dropped them the moment she got bored.

Or so she said. My theory was that she never wanted to get too close. A feeling I knew well.

Twenty minutes later, Madison grinned at me like a Cheshire cat as I frantically blinked, struggling and failing to get my eyes to stop watering. It happened every time I wore eye makeup. Within fifteen minutes, I looked like a damn raccoon. No clue why I kept letting her torture me.

Madison sighed as she tucked a tissue into my hand. "I was really hoping your eyes would cooperate tonight."

"No such luck." I wiped away as much as I could. After a few passes, my eyes stopped freaking out, and I retained a modest amount of the black gunk she lined them with. Better than her last attempt.

I snagged a pair of black wedges from my closet before heading to the door. "Let's get this nightmare over with."

My mom was out at her book club, so I left her a note on our refrigerator chalkboard that I'd gone out with Madison and would be back by curfew. I didn't want to text her because she would ask a thousand questions, and I might have left out the fact that we're going to a party. My mom was pretty reserved, and I already knew it would just turn into an argument. It wasn't as if she even had to worry anyway. I had managed to evade the illicit drugs and alcohol she always rambled on about. In fact, I tended to be DD most of the time.

As I locked my front door, I caught a shadowed figure out of the corner of my eye in the driveway, standing next to the red Eclipse that Parker got for his sixteenth birthday from a car auction. Total steal. Or so I heard.

Madison bumped me with her shoulder and bit her lip in the stupid flirty-bordering-on-sexual way she did when someone caught her eye. "Would it be cheating if I revisit the swim team? I know I swore to one per team, but that boy makes me question my convictions."

"Madison, please—"

"Hey, 4.0." a deep voice called from behind me.

Freaking Parker Hayes.

I tossed my keys into my purse, choking down a groan. All it ever did was egg him on anyway.

"You know calling her smart isn't really an insult, right?" Madison called from my side. "My girl is going to get into any college she wants with grades like hers."

"And I'll get into any college I want, full ride, just because I'm awesome." Parker's hands bounced off his chest in a way that made me think he was challenging the world to go against his word.

Egomaniac.

"Way to flaunt your lack of intelligence, Parker. Don't most colleges have a rule about maintaining a certain GPA while on a sports scholarship? I'll be amazed if you're not working at the local gas station by your second year," I bit back with a sneer.

Parker smirked and leaned against the driver's side door of the car I shared with my mom, blocking my escape. "I love it when you talk nerdy to me. Tell me again why more boys aren't falling all over you with that know-it-all attitude?"

"Can you move?" I crossed my arms over my chest and sent him the best death glare I could muster.

"Where you ladies headed, the library?" He ran a hand through his floppy hair, pushing it off his forehead.

He needed a damn haircut. For some reason I couldn't stop the image of me attacking him with clippers from popping into my head.

I might have done that once when we were kids as retribution for getting gum in my hair. He just laughed after, sucking all the fun out of it.

"We're going to Hunter's party, and I'm already late," I growled, trying and failing to make him understand that I wanted him to go. Far, far away from me.

His mouth popped open in mock surprise. "Well, me too. How about we all carpool? That way I for sure have a safe ride home with Captain DD."

"Go to hell, Parker." I bumped him with my hip, but he didn't budge.

"Man, it's going to take a lot of schmoozing to get me to rate this ride higher than a one star."

"I'm not a damn car service!" I tried to slip my hand behind him, figuring if I could pull the door open, I could dislodge him, but all he did was press his lower back harder onto the door and my hand.

"That's not what I hear. Every time you go to a party, you mom out and end up giving half the class a ride home. I figured I'd jump the line. And since we live so close..." He leaned into me, raising an eyebrow.

"No."

Madison propped the passenger door open, giving me a pleading look. "Just give him a ride, Lil. We're already late."

Late my ass. She just wanted to flirt the whole drive.

I failed to control my irritated groan. All I really wanted

to do was choke the life out of him with my bare hands. Instead, I found myself nodding. "Fine. Whatever."

Parker grinned in his stupid cocky way and slid off my door. I slammed it shut a little harder than I needed to, causing Madison to glance my way. With a giant smile on her face.

Traitor.

Hunter lived right up the road in a new age, schmancy, smart house in a division that even after five years was only partially finished. The developers failed to think about costs beforehand. Not many people could afford the ridiculous price tag. It didn't stop them from tearing down our favorite park though.

Thankfully for me, the proximity meant I only had to endure the flirty conversation between Madison and Parker for a short while. By the time we got to the party, I couldn't wait to get out of the car and get lost in the crowd. Parker kept his digs to a minimum. Maybe he was scared I'd finally snap and send the car off the side of the road. Maybe he was too busy chatting up my traitor of a best friend. In any event, I made it through the drive with minimal homicidal thoughts.

Parker hopped out of the car at the same time as me, bouncing on the balls of his feet before leaning over the door into my personal space. "Thanks for the ride, peaches." He pinched my chin between his thumb and forefinger, and all my suppressed rage toward him boiled up, reaching an internal flash point. "I'll let you know if I need a ride home. That is, if I don't find a hotter option in there."

With that, he jogged up the driveway, leaving me stewing in all the thoughts I wanted to say out loud that he robbed me of.

"We're ditching him, right?" Madison asked as she joined me on the other side of the car.

"Definitely."

She giggled and linked her arm through mine. "I think he has a thing for you."

"Excuse me?" I nearly tripped on the cobblestone leading up to Hunter's front door.

"He totally has the hots for you. All that teasing is repressed lust."

"What did I tell you about saying disgusting things when it comes to Parker?"

"I'm just saying is all."

Madison's terrible commentary came to an abrupt end as we stepped into the house and were swallowed up by the thumping bass of some dance music that sounded the same as every other dance track I had ever heard. Bodies filled the foyer and spilled into every room. Lots of hands-on flirting. The potent smell of alcohol and herbal refreshments.

About as bad as I anticipated.

Madison grabbed my hand and dragged me through the mass of bodies to the kitchen. I had half a mind to dig my heels in and insist on leaving, but the few lusty looks a couple of the guys from our class threw her way convinced me to stay. She would need a DD and possibly a bodyguard to beat them off.

The kitchen island was lined with plastic shot glasses overflowing with a bright-colored substance. In the middle sat a giant glass bowl filled with red liquid and to the side was a keg.

"How do they get all this alcohol?" I shouted over the music.

Madison simply shrugged her shoulders and grabbed

one of the shot glasses. Now that I was closer, I recognized it
as Jell-O.

Classy.

She let the gel fall into her mouth and gave me a wink.
Just as I suspected, she only wanted me to come so she
could get hammered and still have a ride home.

Well, screw that.

Feeling disobedient, I cocked my head and grabbed a
red cup. Her eyebrows shot up as I dipped it into whatever
punch concoction filled the glass bowl. Of course, I didn't
plan on drinking it, I just loved the look on her face when I
did something she didn't expect.

Instead of being mad, though, she bounced up and
down with a squeal and snagged another Jell-O shot.

"Don't tell me Captain DD is drinking?" Parker called
as he strode into the kitchen with one of his jock friends,
Aiden, in tow. I was pretty sure he was the one Madison
had a drunken hookup with right before school let out. By
the way her eyes narrowed, I was almost one-hundred-
percent sure.

I rolled my eyes and took a sip out of pure defiance of
the title I'd been given. You'd think they would all be happy
that I made sure they didn't die or get a DUI on their
record, which would prevent them from playing college
sports. I was also wondering why at a party of this size,
Parker stood by my side instead of finding his next
girl victim.

"You're by the alcohol, genius," Parker said, accurately
reading my thoughts. They must have been plastered all
over my face again. I tend to not be able to hide them very
well around him.

Somehow, it still doesn't scare him off.

"Hey, Madison," Aiden said as he grabbed two Jell-O shots and passed her one.

"Not gonna happen," she yelled over the music.

I watched his smile fall for a millisecond before he shrugged. But that small reaction told me that maybe he liked her a hell of a lot more than he let on. And of all the guys she dated, he was far from the worst. Nice even.

I made a mental note to dig a little deeper. If she felt anything toward him, there was a chance I could persuade her into dating exclusively and give up her man crusade.

Her eyes caught one of the guys from track-and-field two seconds later.

There goes that idea...

"So, DD..." Parker leaned into me, hand settling on my hip.

My molars almost cracked from the pressure I pushed into them in order to keep from landing a kick square in his balls.

"We're gonna play a game of truth or dare downstairs. Want to join?"

"Not if my life depended on it. And get your hand off me."

He smirked, unmoved by the malice in my voice, and pivoted away, taking a sip of his drink.

"Truth or dare?" Madison squealed at my side. "I haven't played that since—"

"You had metal teeth and spoke with a lisp?" Parker cut her off.

I elbowed his side, but he only laughed, his lips hovering over the edge of the cup. Madison flipped him off and clutched my hand with a bit too much enthusiasm.

"Let's play!"

"I'm good." I took another sip of the drink. It wasn't entirely bad, but I needed to break away from the group so I could dump it. I didn't plan on getting drunk, and I wholeheartedly planned on following through being DD for whoever needed it.

"Scared you'll have to admit your feelings for me?" Parker grinned, biting the edge of the cup.

Why did girls fall for that?

"The lust for murder your very presence instills in me?"

"Can't you just talk normal for once?"

"Oh, I'm sorry...let me make it easier for you. Girl no like you. You big jerk."

"Why are you flirting with him?" Madison attempted to whisper in my ear. The shots must have hit her faster than she expected, because half the room heard her, judging by the glances and smirks.

"Yeah, 4.0, why are you flirting with me?" Parker's cocky grin was back.

"I'm not!" I pushed Madison off me, but she only giggled, catching herself on a barstool.

"Let's play." Madison took my hand and jerked me toward the living room. I had been in Hunter's house several times— mostly for parties, once for a study group— so I knew where she was taking me. Down to the man cave, as it's so absurdly named.

I gave in with a growl and allowed her to drag me out of the kitchen. As we passed a table in the hall I set my drink down. No way in hell would I have that handy. Knowing Parker or pretty much any other person at these types of events, they would just dare me to drink the whole thing and then we would be stuck till I sobered up.

Madison let go of me to use the banister for balance as we made our way downstairs. The music wasn't as loud or as crowded down on the lower level. At least I could hear myself think again.

A group of kids huddled on the couch playing some fighting game on the giant, flat-screen TV. Two kids shrieked, playing a rather uncoordinated game of air hockey. Seriously, who has an air hockey table in their house? The group that Madison made her way to sat in a small circle. Some on Lovesacs, others on the floor.

My heart skipped an uneven beat when I realized that I really, really didn't want to do this. I was nowhere near an open book. Madison had been my only close friend since middle school and there was no way I wanted to share anything personal with this group of kids. Which only left me with *dare* and I couldn't even fathom what their drunk brains would come up with.

Madison plopped down on the ground, patting the carpet next to her. Parker and Aiden weren't far behind as I sat cross-legged on the floor. I was happy I chose jeans. Madison looked uncomfortable as hell with her legs off to the side tucked under so that no one got a peek at her goods.

Parker sat across from me, and raised an eyebrow, that I read as a challenge right as the host of the party walked in carrying a clear bottle of what I could only assume was alcohol. He pushed a kid out of the Lovesac to my right and sat down.

"Alright, you all know the rules. If at any point you refuse a truth, you take one shot. You refuse a dare and it's two shots. And I've upped the ante. This is Everclear. It will knock you on your ass quicker than the punch upstairs."

I gulped and narrowed a glare at Madison. "Did you know about this?"

She smirked and straightened her skirt, feigning innocence.

Dead.

I was going to kill her.

Or relieve her of the best friend title.

Both.

Probably both.

"Okay, the last person to have sex gets to start." Hunter looked around the circle of faces until the girl next to Parker cleared her throat.

"About ten minutes ago," she offered, keeping her eyes downcast.

"Nice." Parker sent her a wink, which caused her to laugh and shake her head.

It *really* wasn't that funny. Something told me they hooked up at least once, judging from the red color to her cheeks and the fit of giggles.

"Okay, since Parker likes to be the center of attention..." she said. "Truth or dare?"

"Dare, of course."

"Give me your best striptease for two minutes."

"*Please*, I thought you were more original than that, Em." Parker jumped up and pointed at Hunter. "Give me a good song."

Hunter quickly scrolled through his phone before a thumping beat blared out of his speakers. I buried my face in my clammy hands as Parker started gyrating to the song. Madison whooped from beside me then the rest of the group joined in. I peeked through my fingers long enough to see Parker shirtless and his abs rippling with whatever hip roll he was doing. That would be an image I could never wipe from my head. Even if mental bleach was a thing, I would be scarred.

"Yeah, baby!" Madison hollered.

Pure torture. Worse than I thought when Madison first

demanded I come. It wasn't as if I hated these people—
except Parker—but they had never been my crowd. I was
too introverted for this crap.

The music abruptly ended. "Time," Hunter shouted.

I let out a premature breath as Parker sat back down.
Topless. He fist-bumped Hunter then draped his shirt
around his neck. My eyes jerked away, trying but failing not
to notice his rather nice six-pack.

Nope. Bad thoughts.

I shook my head.

If that was the kind of dare I was in store for, there was
no way in hell I planned on choosing that.

"So, Lily, truth or dare?"

I blinked a few times before I realized Parker was
talking to me. "T-truth." The words flew out before my
brain caught up to who I was speaking to.

He smiled like that was the response he was looking for.
I opened my mouth to change my answer, but it was too
late. "What's the hottest fantasy you have when you go to
solo town?"

"What?" My voice came out in a high-pitched squeal.
Not a sound I think I ever made before. Heat raced up from
my neck to my cheeks, no doubt turning them an unattractive shade of red.

"You heard me."

"I don't even know what that means."

"Come on... Buffin' the muffin. Flicking the bean.
Playin' the clitar."

oh geez

My mouth dropped open at his crude descriptions.
Nope. No way was I answering that.

Hunter shook the bottle of alcohol in the air and
Madison shot me a wide-eyed look. Yeah, I was trapped.

"Pretty much all you want here is masturbation material for yourself, am I right?"

"I do," Hunter called with a grin that immediately prompted whistling from the other guys. "Out with it or take a shot."

I let out a strangled groan. Parker was just trying to make me as uncomfortable as possible. Well, screw him. "No grand fantasy. Just me and the showerhead when the moment strikes."

"Me too!" Em—the girl who got a lap dance—leaned across the divide with a raised hand to give me a high five. I obliged for the sake of moving on.

"That's hot." Hunter took a drink from his cup and motioned to me. "Your turn, Lil."

"Fine, Hunter, truth or dare?"

"Duh. Dare."

I looked around the room for some inspiration. Spying a table of chips over in the corner, I got up and jogged to it. I returned with a jar of salsa in my hand. "Eat this whole thing."

"Child's play!" He snagged the jar from me, nearly spilling his drink all over my shoes in the process. Within an impressive two minutes and minimal gagging, he finished off the jar.

Hunter burped, dragging the back of his hand across his mouth, and focused on Madison. "Truth or dare."

"At the risk of giving y'all more masturbation material, dare."

"Switch your clothes with Lily."

My eyes went wide. "What? No!"

Madison pouted at my side. "Come on, Lil, I don't wanna take a shot of that crap, I have work tomorrow, and I would prefer not to have my head in a toilet."

"Pick someone else."

"That's not the dare." Hunter jiggled the bottle again.

"Please," Madison puppy-whimpered at my side.

It was a low play, and she knew it. I couldn't say no to that stupid face.

"Fine!"

Hunter pointed behind us. "Bathroom's behind you."

I shot him a glare before stepping over to the bathroom with Madison on my heels. Once the door was closed, I turned my glare on her.

"Oh, come on, we'll change before we leave. Your mom will never see you in this."

"And if it ends up on social media?"

Madison opened the door and poked her head out. "No pictures!"

I heard the unmistakable sound of boos from the group as she closed the door. "I'm going to kill you."

Three minutes later, I stared at myself in the mirror, trying my hardest to pull the skirt down. Madison stood several inches shorter than me, and the skirt was already pushing boundaries on her. On me, it looked downright vulgar.

After a series of banging on the door from one of the impatient players, she dragged me out and toward the group. Hunter whistled and Parker's eyebrows shot up so fast they looked like they were about to fly off his head.

"I'm not sitting on the ground in this so you're gonna need to give me that Lovesac." I nudged Hunter with my foot, and he fell out of the beanbag with his hands covering his chest.

"Never thought I'd see the day where you wore anything besides jeans, Lily," Parker said, seeming to have recovered his senses. "I always thought you had tentacles growing under there." He poked my ankle and I kick his hand away.

"Nope, just legs you'll only ever see again in your dreams, so soak it up." I sat carefully in the beanbag, making sure that the skirt didn't rise up any farther.

"My turn!" Madison called and smiled my direction.

"There are other people playing!" I pushed away Hunter as he righted himself and tried to lay his head in my lap.

"Truth or dare, Lil," she said it in her sweet, singsong voice. One that either spelled mayhem or actual sweetness. It could go either way with her.

No way I was choosing truth again, so I figured I would go with dare. She wouldn't screw me over.

"Dare."

Her grin got bigger, and instantly I knew she was leaning toward mayhem. "I dare you to date Parker for the summer."

TWO
Parker

LILY HOLLADAY WAS the bane of my existence. Not because I couldn't stand her—no matter what she thought—but because I couldn't get her out of my head. Dramatic? Definitely. But her stupid green eyes and freckled nose had made a home in the back of my mind since the day I decided girls were more than yucky. Unfortunately, soon after that, Lily decided that she hated my guts. Which led me to spend the better half of high school figuring out how I could turn those feelings around.

It wasn't going well.

Needless to say, I counted my lucky stars when I caught her coming out of the house. I wasn't exactly looking forward to the party, but the second I saw her in that damn green shirt that somehow made her eyes glow, my mood turned around.

I didn't think the night could get any better, but then her best friend, freaking Madison Scott, dared me to date her for the entire summer.

And instantly I had the opening I had been searching for.

Lily's eyes widened, and I thought for a second she was going to choke on her own surprise. I had to admit, even I was pretty shocked Madison went there. The girl had been shamelessly flirting with me all year, and even though I flirted back, there was no chance I would screw up any opportunity with Lily by sleeping with her best friend. Maybe somewhere along the way she picked up on the fact that I had a thing for her friend instead.

In any event, I had never wanted to kiss her more than I did that specific moment.

"Madison, can I talk to you for a second?" Lily's glare darkened as her friend simply shook her head.

"You're up against two shots here, Lil. What's your answer?" Hunter asked with a jiggle of the bottle.

Lily shifted her pleading gaze to me. All I could do was smile. No way in hell an opportunity like that was going to slip through my fingers. She must have read it on my face. After all, we had known each other a long time.

"I'll take the shots," Lily murmured.

My heart plunged to my knees taking all my breath with it. She hated me that much that she couldn't even go along with a stupid dare for the summer?

Without thinking, I turned to her. "You've never been one to turn down a dare." I dragged my thumb across my lower lip. She narrowed her eyes into slits, her own hand flying up to rest on her chin. Right on her scar.

"Lil, come on." Madison tilted her head. "Two shots of that and you'll end up in the hospital."

Madison was right, which was precisely why Hunter had chosen it. He got entertainment either way. A forced truth or dare and if someone refused, he got to see them with borderline alcohol poisoning, which was enough ammo to torture them for the rest of high school.

"And a summer of dating him and I'll end up in jail for manslaughter." Lily stabbed an accusatory finger in my direction.

Geez, it wasn't as if I was in on it. I was just as shocked as her. Ecstatic. But still shocked.

"You don't have to do it," I found myself saying. I don't know where it came from, but if she actually planned to risk alcohol poisoning over a dare, then I needed to stop it.

Her pleading look turned back into a glare. "Oh why? So I can hear about this for the rest of the year? You know what, fine, I'll date you for the summer. On one condition— you do *not* get to date anyone else. If I have to suffer, then so do you, and a summer of celibacy seems like the perfect trade."

I rolled my eyes. "Fine, Lil, whatever you say."

Little did she know I hadn't hooked up with anyone for a year. The last time made me physically ill, especially when I found out Lily saw.

Yeah. A story for another time.

She threw me one last dirty look before getting up and stomping up the stairs with the most dramatic flair I'd ever seen from her. I had a hard time keeping my eyes off her long legs. She should wear skirts more often.

"I guess the game is over," Hunter called as he made his way upstairs. "Who wants to go swimming?"

The rest of the group jumped up and followed him. Madison lingered, beaming at me as if I owed her the world as I slipped my shirt on.

"What?"

"You're welcome," she replied as she got up, adjusting the green top that didn't look nearly as mouthwatering on her. "I guessed you had a thing for her. I mean why else would you repeatedly turn me down?" She emphasized her point by sliding her hand down her side. "I'm giving you this opening, but if you hurt my girl, all the deaths she has imagined for you over the years will pale in comparison."

"Yes, ma'am." I mock saluted her then slid my arm around her lower back. "Should we go find my girlfriend?"

Madison giggled as she walked away.

My summer was already starting out better than I planned.

We found Lily in the kitchen staring at the Jell-O shots as if she couldn't decide if they would help her or not. The girl always had a calculating expression on her face, running through the various repercussions to her actions. I don't think she's ever stopped to just have fun. Not since we were kids.

Madison smacked a shot glass out of her hand the second Lily reached for it. "Let's go, Lil."

Lily's mouth fell open in shock as the shot glass hit the ground and splattered the cabinets in red goop. Good thing no one was in its path. All it would have done was start a drunken argument if someone got dirty.

Lily opened her mouth to respond before her eyes locked on me hovering behind Madison. "What is *he* doing here?" she hissed. Only it came out as more of a yell and several people in the kitchen turned in our direction.

"Come on." Madison gripped her upper arm and steered her toward the front door. "Let's call an Uber. I've had several drinks and apparently you can't hold even the tiniest bit of liquor."

"I am *not* drunk! And why is he here?" Lily spun out of Madison's grasp the second they stepped out onto the porch. "I seriously can't believe you. I'm not the one who's all hot and wet for him, so why did you give me that ridiculous dare, huh?"

I *knew* Madison had the hots for me.

Madison gave a small shrug and tried to loop her arm through Lily's. Lily shoved her away, face red from either repressed anger or alcohol. I wasn't sure how much of that punch she drank or if we got to her before she inhaled a Jell-O shot.

Madison narrowed her eyes, and I was certain I was three seconds away from witnessing a catfight between two girls who have never fought a day in their friendship. I threw up my hands and stepped between them, feeling as if I was trying to reason with terrorists.

"Why don't we go get some food, huh? Dick's on me."

"Fitting restaurant for someone like you," Lily muttered under her breath.

"I love Dick's!" Madison shouted, then squealed when she noticed the group of kids hanging out on the porch twisted in her direction. "Burgers, you pervs!"

The kids laughed as they turned back to their conversation. Madison huffed and shoved her hair out of her face, looking far more flushed than she did when we left the house. "What do you say, Lil? I think those shots had more kick than I was expecting, and I could use some greasy food to soak up the alcohol. I'll be grounded all summer if I go home drunk. Again."

Lily chewed on her lower lip for a few seconds before groaning and giving in with a nod. She leveled a glare in my direction. "But I'm only going because Madison needs me. Don't get any sick and twisted ideas about this being a date."

"First of all," I took a step toward her. "I would never take a girl on a date to Dick's. I'm classier than that. And second," I pushed the boundaries of her personal space, catching her off guard and allowing myself time to sink my hand in her purse to retrieve her car keys. "I'm driving." I shook her keys in the air, narrowly missing her grabbing hand.

"Give me my keys, Parker. I've seen you drive, and I would prefer not to die in a car accident."

"I got a perfect score on my driving test, thank you very much. And I don't know how much of that punch you ingested, so I'd rather drive us home."

"You drank it too!" She pointed a long, delicate finger in my face and once again made a grab for the keys.

"It was just a Coke. I have to help my dad with something tomorrow morning. I didn't want to be hungover."

"So why did you bum a ride off me, then?" she whined and stuck her bottom lip out in the most adorable pout I had ever seen.

"Because Madison was with you." I decided to go with a lie instead of laying all my cards out on the table, and telling her it was because I wanted to spend the extra few minutes with her.

"I hate you," she growled and stalked over to her car.

I hate to see you go, but I love to see you walk away in that skirt.

"I'll turn that hate into love by the end of the summer, Holladay."

Madison crossed her arms over her chest and smirked at me. "You better try a hell of a lot harder than that. If you think irritating her into submission will work, you might as well go and down that whole bottle of Everclear. It will be an easier death than what she'll have in store for you."

I smiled and draped my arm across her shoulders. "All I heard is that I have a chance."

"You're an idiot." Madison shoved me off and stumbled toward the car.

⁂

Fifteen minutes later, we sat in Lily's car, enjoying our food. Well, Madison and I did. Lily sulked in the back seat, picking the smallest bites off the patty and sipping on her shake every now and then.

She hadn't said a word since I got in the car. Not even to tell me what she wanted to eat. At least the menu wasn't extensive. But I had to think back really hard to remember what her favorite shake was. My dad had taken us here at least once a month when we were kids. Back when we were friends. Lily always ordered the strawberry shake and proceeded to dip her fries into it before eating them.

I've tried it and it's disgusting.

I glanced in the rearview mirror and caught her popping a fry into her mouth, sans shake.

Guess she grew out of that.

"This isn't awkward at all," Madison mumbled before taking a huge bite of her burger.

I laughed because it was true. Normally I'd be all over Lily, making her as uncomfortable as possible, because at least it was some kind of reaction. But Madison's words kept coming back. I wouldn't get Lily to like me by irritating her into submission. Digging myself out of the hole I created would require some effort to not be a dick.

Dick.

Dick's.

This was the perfect place for me.

I laughed and took a sip of my shake.

"What's so funny?" Lily demanded from behind me.

"Nothing." I bit into my burger. I could have told her she was right about that comment, but that's not the impression I wanted to leave her with. I could be more than a dick. Sure, it was my reigning personality trait, but deep down there was more.

There had to be, right?

"Can we go home now?" Lily tossed her food into the bag before setting it down on the floorboard.

"I'm still drunk," Madison complained from the passenger seat. The alcohol seemed to hit her full force on the drive over.

"You can sleep over," Lily offered and pulled out her phone. "My mom won't be home for another hour. Which is good because I'm still wearing your damn clothes."

"And looking smoking hot might I add." Madison sent her an over-the-top wink then turned to me. "Tell your girl-friend she looks hot."

Lily groaned.

I liked drunk Madison. With her as my cheerleader, I might actually have a shot.

"Lily, you look smoking hot in that skirt."

"Bite me, asshole."

"Ouch." Madison reached for the bag that Lily threw her food in and tossed her wrappers in. "That's no way to talk to your boyfriend."

"Keep it up and I'll send your drunk ass home to be grounded."

"Okay. Fine. Whatever." Madison held her hands up in defeat but not before sending me a wink.

"I saw that," Lily grumbled from behind me.

I chucked my wrappers into the bag then started the car. Looked like I might have to rely heavily on Madison to turn Lily around. If that was the case, I couldn't have her grounded for the whole summer.

Interstate 5 was relatively clear for a Friday night and I pulled up into Lily's driveway within twenty minutes. Just in time for Madison to gag and thrust open the door to spew her burger and God knows what else all over the pavement.

Great.

Lily wasted no time jumping out of the car to help her friend. I hopped out and rounded the back of the car. We needed to get her inside pronto, before Lily's mom got home or my dad looked outside to check on the commotion. He was a known night owl, and I could just imagine how well it would go over with all of our parents that we arrived home with a very intoxicated Madison.

I lifted Madison up into my arms and nodded toward the door. "Get the door, I've got her."

Lily blinked at me a few times as if she couldn't believe I was helping before letting go of her friend's hand and making her way to the front steps.

The house was dark and dead quiet as we entered. It was a good thing, I guessed. At least that meant her mom wasn't home yet.

Lily pointed to the stairs as she simultaneously set her purse down and flicked on the entryway light. I didn't need her direction. I had been in her house plenty of times when we were younger. Unless she moved her bedroom, I knew exactly where it was. First door on the right at the top of the stairs. Coincidently, it happened to face my bedroom.

Madison groaned in my arms, letting her head loll to the side. I really hoped she didn't barf on me. That would be a little harder to sneak past my dad. And the last thing I needed was to get grounded.

I set Madison down on Lily's bed and took a cursory glance around the room, looking for a trash can or something I could leave by the bed in case she hurled again. I couldn't help but notice that Lily's room looked nothing like it did when we were kids. Of course, I hadn't been in her room for at least four years, but I remembered it being a lot more pink.

The pink was gone, though. The walls had been painted off-white with a teal accent wall behind her bed. Her comforter matched with a teal-and-white paisley print. All of her stuffed animals and Barbies were gone. There were no unicorn or boy-band posters. Those had been replaced by hanging shelves lined with books and picture frames devoted to her and Madison.

The only thing she seemed to have kept from her childhood was a pair of beaded curtains that separated her closet from the room. Their neon flowers were tied off to the side and out of the way of the door. I smirked as I took them in. I bought those for her ninth birthday. I couldn't believe she kept them.

Lily stormed into the room carrying a pan and a glass of water. "My mom just pulled in. You should go."

I gave her a nod as she set the glass on the nightstand and the bucket on the floor. I really wanted to stay and badger her about the fact that she kept one of my gifts. But I didn't need Ms. Holladay coming in and seeing me in a room with a scantily dressed Lily and a drunk Madison. We'd all get grounded, then and it would ruin the entire summer.

And that would just ruin all of my plans.

THREE
Lily

THE AIR MATTRESS squeaked under me as I rolled over. The light was muted outside my window, just past dawn, which meant I had slept maybe three hours.

Parker's sudden appearance at the bottom of my stairs had stalled my mom enough to cover up Madison and gave me time to change out of her clothes. I didn't think my mom believed for one second that Madison had eaten something bad at the restaurant we "went to." But she seemed way more interested in discussing why Parker was in our house to press too hard.

That was a delightful conversation. My one semester of theater really helped sell the idea that I didn't absolutely loathe Parker and that he was just so helpful when Madison fell ill in the driveway. The combo lie would make it a total of seven lies I had told my mom in my seventeen years on Earth. The first one had been about the piece of candy I had stolen from a gas station when I was six. My latest, before the whole Madison ordeal, was that my father leaving didn't bother me. oh damn

There was a high chance the lies would continue to accumulate as I attempted to hide the fact that Parker and I would be fake dating the entire summer thanks to Miss Pukes-a-Lot.

Speaking of Madison, she better be one good liar, or her moms would have her doing community service at the local animal shelter instead of spending lazy days with me.

And judging by the way Parker acted after that stupid dare, I would need her as a buffer. Even my own damn mom was salivating over the prospect of us spending time together. She'd practically had our wedding mapped out since we were kids. I'd burst that bubble long ago when we stopped hanging out every day but seeing him in our house might have ignited a new fire. Or threw accelerant on the old smoldering one.

I draped an arm over my eyes in an attempt to block out the light. He was the real reason I couldn't sleep. I'd been ready to wring his stupid neck after the whole night, but then he went and did something weirdly nice and helped me put Madison to bed. I hadn't seen him do anything remotely selfless in, like, forever. So, with that kind gesture, my foolish brain slid down a rabbit hole, most of which revolved around him. Him and all the fun times we had together before he decided I was no longer worth his time. Then, when I finally fell asleep, I had a nightmare where his full and infuriatingly dreamy lips were all over mine. And in my twisted head, I liked it. Okay, more than liked it.

So, all night I tossed and turned with Parker dominating both my waking and sleeping thoughts. Round and round in a circle until I wanted to cry, because awake me still hated him but dream me seemed to have other ideas.

Yeah, I was never going back to sleep. Maybe never again.

What I really needed was a long, hot shower and an extra-large, almond-milk, caramel macchiato from my favorite coffee joint. It was this tiny little shack in a parking lot that housed mostly home-improvement stores, but it was the best coffee I'd ever had. Something about pulling their own shots and then smothering it all in ooey-gooey caramel. Seriously, angels sang every time I took a sip. Rainbows appeared. My general hatred for everyone lessened. Believe it or not, that was the biggest miracle out of the three.

With a sigh, I rolled off the side of the mattress and attempted not to take the blankets with me. I despised the blow-up bed. Next time Madison got trashed beyond belief, I was making her sleep on it.

The house was quiet as I made my way across the hall to the bathroom. I had about an hour of peace before my mom woke up to get ready for work. The company she worked for had been hosting an event twice a month on Saturdays for local kids. It was meant to get them into science and technology industries at a young age. They geared it toward girls, but everyone brought their kids. With lectures and structure, it pretty much meant parents could dump them there for a couple of hours and have a free Saturday.

Don't ask me how a realty office got involved in science. I never understood it. But it worked.

I cranked the water up as high as I could handle and stripped as it warmed up. As I got undressed, my mind drifted to Parker. Again. I had to come up with a way out of the dare or he would spend the whole summer break torturing me. The logical answer was to find him an easy, gullible girl to distract him—kind of like a laser pointer with a cat—but I shot myself in the foot when I banned him from dating other girls.

I was just trying to piss him off, but instead I shoved myself into a corner.

The hot water rolled down my back as I stepped into the shower.

God, it felt good.

It was difficult to stay pissy at the situation as the steam swirled around me and the heat loosened my stiff muscles. I was never sleeping on that blow-up bed again. I was pretty sure my mom bought it sometime in the '90s. There were several glue-on patches that did little to stop the slow loss of air. I was amazed I didn't end up on the floor in a heap of deflated plastic in the middle of the night.

Thirty minutes later. Scrubbed clean. Sorta awake. And I still had no answer about Parker.

Stupid Parker. He had made torturing me his favorite pastime over the past four years. Impeccable timing, too. The summer my dad walked out on my mom and me. Great friend, right? I kind of thought since he had been my friend since we were two, he would be there for me. But no, he decided that was the best time to drop me and move on to cooler friends, all while doing his damnedest to make sure I remained in my dark hole of sadness.

I had sworn that summer that I never wanted him in my life ever again. And there he was, four years later, trying to reinsert himself like a puzzle piece that had been trimmed to fit instead of the piece that belonged there. The saddest part about the whole thing was that our friendship ended the summer I planned on telling him I was in love with him.

Gag me, right?

But it was the truth.

Dumb, naive me had once been in love with the jerk.

Good thing I saved myself the embarrassment and kept that to myself.

Madison groaned and gave me a small wave as I entered my bedroom. Her messy, bed head poked out from under my pillow, squinting at her cell.

"Parentals?" I asked as I reached for my brush.

"Five missed calls and twenty texts between the both of them. Remind me to thank your mom later."

"Do they at least believe you were sick?"

"Judging from the start of the chain, yes. Toward the end, not so much."

I set the brush down and plopped on the edge of the bed causing Madison to groan again. Served her right for getting so wasted. "How can they show up for this when they couldn't care less how you dress or where you go?"

"Drinking is a big deal in my family. It's like their one rule."

I slid my hand under the covers and popped one of her toes. She squealed and tucked her feet up. "Think you'll get grounded?"

"They can't ground me if I avoid them until all traces of alcohol are gone."

"I think you managed that last night in my driveway."

"Oh, God." Madison lifted the pillow to peek at me. "Please tell me I didn't throw up all over Parker."

I wrinkled my nose in disgust. "You're worried about Parker? What about my shoes? I have bits of hamburger plastered all over the fabric."

"Shut up, you do not!" She threw the pillow at me, which I caught and tucked under my forearms on my lap.

"I expect you to get them cleaned. They're my favorite pair."

"I'm never going to a party again."

"Not until the next one, right?"

She grinned, then sat up slowly, gripping my arm and wincing. "Is your mom up yet? Maybe a shower will help this pounding headache."

"You have, like, twenty minutes."

"Perfect." She threw her legs over the side of the bed

and wobbled slightly once they touched the floor. "Can I live here if my moms find out what really happened last tonight?"

"No, not a chance."

Madison giggled as she stumbled out of the bedroom. I breathed out a sigh of relief. She seemed more like herself. I've seen her drink before, but I've never seen her puking her guts out because of it. If Parker hadn't been so calm about the whole thing, I might have been tempted to call 911 and have her taken in for alcohol poisoning.

Parker.

Why couldn't I get him out of my head? I threw my pillow against the wall then grabbed a pair of jeans and a hoodie. I figured I would have time to go run and pick up coffee before my mom left, and I took Madison home. Maybe I could order her a tea instead of coffee. I wasn't sure, but judging from her reaction to simply walking, her stomach might not be up for the whole milk-and-sugar thing.

I snagged my purse from the floor and made my way outside. Mr. Jones across the street was already deep into his Saturday morning yardwork ritual. He had the best lawn on the block, something he took a lot of pride in. If it meant getting up at the crack of dawn and staying out there sweating and laboring for most of the day, I would settle for Astroturf or just throw a bunch of bark down and call it a day.

I was so busy admiring his hard work that I didn't notice the person leaning up against my car until I almost bumped into them.

"Sorry, I—" My eyes narrowed on Parker, and I had the sudden urge to punch him square in the gut. All the nice things I thought about him helping Madison evaporated the second I was faced with this cocky smirk. "What do you want?"

He grabbed a drink carrier that housed three beverages, including one that looked suspiciously like my favorite coffee, off the roof of the car. I read the label on the cup and my eyes narrowed farther.

"What is this?"

"Coffee. Well, coffee for you and your mom and a tea for Madison. Judging from her gastrointestinal acrobatics, I didn't think milk would settle too well."

I stared at him in disbelief. Those were my exact thoughts. "I was just headed to get coffee."

"Now you don't have to." He held the carrier out in the space between us as I continued to stare at him.

"What did you do, spit in it?"

He chuckled and cocked his head. "Why would I do that?"

"Why would you buy me coffee at all?" I countered.

"Can't a boyfriend buy his girlfriend coffee?"

My stomach churned, and I had the overwhelming urge to do what Madison did the previous night. All over his nice, white shoes.

Of course, he would make a spectacle. It was asking too much to go even a day, one day, without him being a jerk. There was no doubt in my mind that he already had a good laugh about this with his jock friends. He probably made bets on how far he could go with me.

"I can get my own coffee."

"Lil, just take the damn coffee and say thank you." He pressed the carrier into my stomach, giving me no choice but to grab it or risk it spilling all over me.

"What are you doing up so early?" I asked in an attempt to break the sudden tension between us.

He leaned against my car, running a hand through his damp hair. "My dad has a strict off-season schedule for my swimming. He doesn't want me to get lazy during the summer. You should see my diet plan." He mock shuddered, adding a gag in for extra effect.

When did Mr. Hayes get so strict about his swimming? Sure, he encouraged Parker, but most of the time he was busy at work and missed the meets. Mrs. Hayes was always there, though. And me. Right by her side with giant glitter signs to embarrass him. This was, of course, back when we liked each other.

"Anyway, I have the rest of the afternoon to myself. Do you have any plans?" Parker asked with a somewhat hopeful expression on his face.

No, I didn't. But I couldn't let him know that. He had something terrible planned. I could feel it.

"Yeah, I'm helping my mom at some work event."

"The kids-in-science thing? Since when do you help her with that?"

"Since none of your business."

My mom decided that exact moment was the perfect time to come out onto the porch for the paper that had been sitting there all week. Yeah, something smelled fishy. She was even up earlier than normal.

"Hey, Ms. Holladay." Parker waved and gave her a bright smile. Full teeth and all.

Kiss ass.

"I told you last night, call me Jan." The expression on my mom's face could only be described as jubilant.

"I brought you some coffee." He motioned to the carrier I held and for some reason I tried to turn my body to conceal it as if it was some kind of contraband.

"Oh, how sweet! I'm about to make pancakes. Would you like to join us?"

"Since when do you cook breakfast?" I asked before Parker could answer.

"Since one of the girls gave me a great blueberry recipe last night at book club."

Book club. I snorted. In reality, it was just an excuse to get together and drink a bunch of wine. I hadn't seen my mom read a book since she was reading me Dr. Seuss.

"Pancakes sound amazing," Parker called from behind me.

I couldn't mask the rage on my face as I turned around to glare at him. Since when did they get so buddy-buddy? He talked to her for maybe five minutes the previous night.

"Parker can't have pancakes. He's on a strict diet for swimming," I answered for him.

Parker gave me a dirty look to which I smirked. He was the idiot that let that information slip. Now I had something to use against him and, if push came to shove, tell his dad. If it meant keeping Parker away from me, I wasn't above cheap shots.

"Good thing these are low carb," my mom called and stepped back into the house.

Now it was Parker's turn to smirk. "Really, Lil? Going for the cheap shot? Why don't you want me to have breakfast with you? Scared your mom will love me? I can't wait to tell her we're dating."

My mouth popped open. "You wouldn't."

He shrugged and skirted around me, headed for the door. I couldn't let this happen. Me dating Parker was a dream come true for my mom. I had no idea why she loved him so much. She would literally jump for joy.

I caught Parker's forearm as he reached for the door-knob. "Please don't tell her we're dating."

"So little Ms. 4.0 lies to her mom, huh?"

"It would be a lie to tell her we're dating."

"But we are."

"No, we're not!" I closed my eyes and took a deep, cleansing breath, trying to rein in my irritation. "It's a stupid dare, that's it. Why would you tell her something like that?"

"Because, if your mom thinks we're dating, then you won't try to back out." His cocky grin turned mischievous, much like it did when we were kids and about to do something that would end with a trip to the ER.

Okay, so he had a point. If my mom was harping on me and doing everything she could to get us together to go out, it would make it harder to avoid him.

"Why do you care so much about a stupid dare, huh? Is torturing me *that* fun?"

Something flashed in his eyes, an emotion I swear I had never seen there before. Regret maybe? Whatever it was, disappeared the second he blinked.

"I'm just holding up my side of the dare. Hunter will never let me live it down if I back out. Unfortunately, that requires you to go along with it." His large hand came down on my shoulder. "Live a little, Holladay. Spend the summer with me, and I'll teach you how to have fun again."

"I know how to have fun." I shook his hand off and he laughed.

"Sure, Lil. Keep telling yourself that." With that, he entered my house, leaving me staring after his retreating back until the front door closed.

FOUR
Lily

WE ALL SAT around the suddenly clean kitchen table—one normally used to store mail and clothes that needed repairing—eating Mom's weird healthy pancakes. They didn't taste that bad. I'm more of a smother-carbs-in-as-much-sugar-as-you-can girl, but if she never told me they were nutritious, I might have been fooled.

Madison passed on the pancakes, sipping on her tea instead. The tea I meant to get her, but Parker showed up with in a total best-friend-stealing-thunder moment.

I still had no clue how he knew my favorite coffee place, let alone my favorite coffee. Or why he went out of his way to do it. At first, I thought he felt bad for the whole agreeing-to-date-me-against-my-will thing and had come to apologize. Two servings of pancakes later, I realized that was never going to happen.

"Aren't you going to be late for work?" I asked my mom, interrupting some story about Parker and me when we were kids. I'm sure it was just super adorable, but I needed the madness to end and for Parker to get the hell out of my house. Preferably before he told her about the dare.

My mom sighed. "I guess you're right. We should have you and your dad over for dinner sometime this week. It's been so long since we've had a proper conversation with how busy we both are."

"That would be—"

"He can't," I blurted out, cutting off Parker mid-sentence.

My mom shot me a wide-eyed look that was mom code for *what the hell is your problem? You're being so rude.*

"Lil is right. I just remembered that we're going up to the lake in a couple of days."

"Your dad still owns that? Gosh, so many great memories up there."

Parker nodded and grinned in my direction. "The lake house was always a great time. And I just had a crazy idea. What if we take Lily up with us?"

My mom awed and clapped her hands together, and Madison nearly spit out her tea.

I swear my stomach almost pole-vaulted out of my body. Going to the lake house with Parker? Nuh-uh. No way.

"I can't."

"Why not, sweetie? It's not like you have any big plans. You're not even working this summer."

I glanced over at Madison, pleading with my eyes. She shrugged and took a drink of her tea. At this rate, she would be lucky if she still donned the best-friend title by the end of the summer with the amount of times she had thrown me under the bus.

"I just...can't." A lame response, but it was the only thing I could think of. I couldn't come out and admit that spending a week secluded with Parker would make me either kill him or kiss him.

Most likely kill him and throw him in the lake.

"Come on, Lil." Parker bumped me with his shoulder.

"It will be fun. Jet Skis. Boating. You might even get some color."

"That sounds like a fun way to spend your summer," my mom said as she stood and picked up everyone's plates. "How long will you be up there for?"

"Just a week. It's all my dad could get off."

"Well, if your father is okay with it, I'm okay with it."

Parker grinned triumphantly. "So, Holladay, you in?"

"She's in," Madison answered for me.

What was it with everyone deciding my life was theirs to meddle in?

"Great." Parker stood and made his way to the door, presumably before I could come up with a reason to say no. "I'll let my dad know. We planned on leaving late Tuesday, but we can drive up together earlier. Get an extra day."

"Sounds good," my mom answered.

My mouth dropped open, and I glanced around the room confused as to what was going on. Had I up and disappeared? Because that was the only explanation as to why not a single person heard or responded to the fact that I had no interest in going to the lake with Parker.

The second the door clicked shut I turned to my mom. "Seriously?"

"What?" she asked, as she scraped the scraps of food into the trash.

"I don't want to go to the lake with Parker and his dad."

"Why not?"

"Yeah, why not?" Madison chimed in. "If I didn't have to work, I'd be all over that."

"Most kids would kill to spend the week at a lake house having fun on the water."

"I'm not most kids!" I slammed my palm onto the table, making both Madison and my mom jump.

"What has gotten into you, Lily Evelynn Holladay?"

Not the full name.

My body heated from anger, and I turned away. I had never gotten around to telling my mom how much I hated Parker and how much he loved making my life a living hell. She had been so close with his mom before she died, I kind of felt bad tarnishing her perfect, little Parker picture.

Now I wished I had told her everything.

"Fine. I'll go."

"Don't sound too happy about it."

I finished my coffee then tossed it in the trash. He had even buttered her up with coffee. The boy was good. Now I looked like an ungrateful brat. "I have to take Madison home."

"I'll be home by four. If you want, we can go shopping for a new bathing suit. I can't recall the last time you got a new one."

"Sure," I mumbled as I headed for the door.

My summer hadn't even begun, and already I couldn't wait for school to start back up.

<hr />

I lay on my bed staring at the ceiling with a book sprawled on my stomach, willing myself to do something, anything. I hadn't spoken to Madison the entire drive to her house. It didn't stop her from trying to talk to me, though. Either I wasn't putting out strong enough vibes that I was pissed at her, or she didn't care.

All she talked about was how much she wished she could come with me and that if I wanted, she would go with me to pick out a smoking-hot bikini that would make Parker drool. Her words, not mine.

If she had been feeling one hundred percent, I would have let her have it. But judging from the pale coloring to her face, the alcohol was still wreaking havoc on her body.

One could only hope she learned her lesson, though I highly doubted it.

After I dropped her off, I came straight home, intent of figuring a way to get out of the lake trip. I wasn't above faking the flu. Summer flus weren't unheard of. I looked it up.

When I ran into Mr. Hayes, and he told me how delighted he was to have me come along, any plan I had blew up. After seeing how animated he was, I didn't have the heart to tell him no. What was with our parents? It was as if Parker and I hanging out together was the best present they could have received.

If they knew how much of an ass Parker was, they might have felt differently.

I rolled onto my side and let out a sigh. I couldn't even concentrate on reading, and reading was normally my favorite escape. It started when my parents were still together, and they would fight late at night when they thought I was asleep. The noise made it impossible to sleep —to think—so I put on some music and read. I didn't have to focus on how crappy my life was when I could fall into another world and lose myself in it.

Parker had managed to ruin even my favorite pastime.

Figured.

I tossed my book on my pillow and reached for my phone as it dinged with a notification.

I expected it to be from Madison. Maybe she came to her senses and sent me an apology text. When I clicked my phone on, I was greeted with a text from a number I didn't recognize.

. . .

Unknown: I'm bored

I cocked my head and reread the phone number. It was local. Anyone worth talking to at school was already saved in my phone. With the assumption it was a wrong number I replied.

Me: Who is this?

The reply was almost instant.

Unknown: Wow. R u dating so many guys that u can't keep us straight?

My stomach sank, and I sat up scowling at the phone. Could Parker not leave me alone for more than a few minutes? It was bordering on stalkerish behavior.

Before replying, I saved him to my contacts so that I would know to avoid him in the future.

Me: No, but any guy worth talking to would have already been saved in my phone.

. . .

Parker: Ouch. U really know how to cut down a guy's ego.

I rolled my eyes but didn't reply. I figured he would get the hint and leave me the hell alone, but a few minutes later my phone chimed. It chimed again three minutes after that.

Morbid curiosity got the best of me, and I reached for my phone.

Parker: Wanna go to the movies? There's nothing good but we can eat junk food and make fun of it.

Parker: I know ur home. Ur car is in the driveway.

And there lay the problem with living right next door to a boy that drove you insane. I couldn't pretend I wasn't home. He would know. Again, very stalkerish.

Truth be told, I was bored, and that did sound kind of fun. If he wasn't the bane of my existence and I hadn't imagined three different ways to kill him—in one day—I might have agreed.

Instead, I put my phone on silent and decided that a midafternoon nap was in order. After that, I would need to figure out how to avoid him for the next couple of days.

FIVE
Parker

Lily never responded to my text the other night and for the past couple of days had managed to evade me every time I was home. According to her Instagram, she decided to stay the night at Madison's house and volunteer at the animal shelter during the day.

My gut reaction was to volunteer as well but decided against it. Doing something I had never done before would tip her off. I would have her to myself for the next week and planned on using that time to win her over. I didn't want to start that with her more irritated than she already was.

My dad had talked to her mom on Sunday, and together they agreed that I could drive Lily up and my dad would meet us later that night.

So, at twelve on the dot I walked up her front steps and knocked on the front door. I half expected her not to be home or to feign some sickness, but to my surprise, she opened the door wearing the shortest pair of shorts I had ever seen on her. Sure, she matched it with an oversize Batman shirt, but still, I was taken aback. Lily chose that moment to toss her bag at me.

I almost didn't catch it, and once I did I wished I hadn't. It wasn't big, maybe the size of a gym bag, but she must have had it loaded down with bowling balls. I let out a grunt as it connected with my stomach. I stumbled back, as it almost sent me down the front steps.

Lily didn't even try to hide her amusement as she locked up the door and strode past me. I trailed after her, swinging her bag up onto my shoulder.

"It's about a two and a half hour drive. I got us a bunch of snacks."

"Cool." She rounded my car, never once glancing in my direction.

So, she planned on icing me out the entire drive. Awesome. I tossed her bag into the open trunk then slammed it shut with a little too much force. The car dipped under the weight and Lily shot me an amused look as she slipped into the passenger seat.

She had her earbuds in by the time I climbed behind the wheel. Her gaze darted to the side, effectively cutting me off.

I sighed and started the car. She really was going to make this difficult, wasn't she?

Forty-five minutes into the drive, four radio stations, and enough junk food to cause a stomachache had me going out of my mind. I had never made the trip to the lake house alone, and with Lily in her sensory deprivation chamber that's what I was doing.

I tapped my fingers on the steering wheel to the beat of the song blaring from the speakers and concentrated on the road. I hadn't been to the lake since my mother died. My dad went up every year, but I always came up with some excuse. He was floored when I told him that not only was I going, but Lily was coming too. It used to be a big thing with both of our families spending a week up there every summer and a couple of Christmases here and there.

But the same year that Lily's dad left, my mom had a sudden heart attack and passed away. The lake house lost all of its light, and I avoided it like the plague from then on.

No clue what got into me when I blurted that out at the breakfast table. But the way her mom's eyes lit up, as if she was reliving all the good memories, solidified my plan, and I had a hard time backpedaling.

The moment I got in the car, however, I felt all those memories punch me in the gut. Sure, they were happy, but they were also a reminder of things I would never get back. Like my mother or Lily's friendship. This whole forcing her to date me suddenly seemed like the worst idea.

I reached over the center console and yanked out Lily's earbuds.

"Hey!" she protested and reached for them, but I pulled away.

"I was just thinking..."

"Did that hurt?" Lily tried to take back her headphones again, but I held on tight.

"Cut the sass. I'm trying to tell you something."

She crossed her arms over her chest and turned toward me with a deep-set frown on her face. "What?"

I focused my attention back on the road, so we didn't crash. "I think you were right. It's kinda messed up to force you to fake-date me for the summer. After this week, I'll drive you home and we can just drop it."

Lily scoffed, and I turned my head briefly to see her glaring at me.

Not the reaction I expected.

"So, what, you let me off the hook, and then I get teased

about it the rest of the summer and senior year? Yeah, I don't think so, Hayes."

"No, that's not what I meant." God, she could be so damn stubborn. She didn't want to date me, but she didn't want to not date me either.

"Uh-huh." She tugged on her headphones, but I tugged harder, pulling them free from her phone and whipping the end into the windshield.

"Dude, what the hell?" she yelled and shoved my shoulder.

The car swerved, and I quickly righted it. Apparently safe driving was not something her mother taught her.

"Hey, driving here!"

"Hey, annoyed here."

"Lily, I'm giving you an out."

"Sure you are."

"I'm serious. We can tell everyone we went through with it if you want, but whatever... you're free."

I felt her eyes on me. "Just like that?"

"Just like that."

"Why don't I believe you?"

"Because you have trust issues?"

Lily laughed her first genuine laugh with me in years. I smiled, feeling lighter but didn't press the subject any further. If she needed us not to be dating, that was fine. I would have to win her over some other way. And I had a week to figure out how.

We spent the last stretch of the drive in relative silence. She didn't attempt to talk to me, but she didn't put her earbuds back in. Somewhere along the way, she started up a game of punch buggy, but I had a hunch it was her way of getting out her aggression toward me. It seemed to have worked, because by the time I pulled up the dirt road that led to my family's lake house, she was laughing and singing along to the radio.

I almost felt bad cutting off her rendition of Ed Sheeran. It had gotten pretty animated.

Lily leaned to the side and stared up at the three-story house that had been in my family since before I was born.

"Wow. Did it get bigger?"

I smirked, holding back the comment I really wanted to say. It would only piss her off. "Must be you," I said instead, stepping out onto the gravel.

It smelled exactly how I remembered.

"Is it weird to say it smells the same?" Lily asked from behind me.

"No, I was thinking the same thing." We were too much alike sometimes.

"Hmm." She strode past me, headed toward the front door as if she owned the place. Judging from her purse, and nothing else, dangling from her hand. She also left her bag for me to lug into the house.

As punishment, I left her to wait on the front porch as I pulled the bags out of the car, taking my sweet-ass time. A few times I heard an exasperated huff, but that only spurred me on. By the end of the thorough recheck of my bag, mostly just to irritate her, footsteps sounded on the driveway.

Lily rounded the back of the car, eyebrows arched when she took me in, bent over my bag, settling my shirts back in.

"Really?"

"What?" I asked, struggling to keep amusement out of my voice.

"I'm standing up there waiting for you to let me in. You could have done whatever you're doing inside."

I zipped up the bag and stood. "But it's so beautiful out."

"I have to pee!" She threw her hands up in the air and this time I couldn't stop my laughter.

"You're an ass!" she yelled and stomped her way back up the driveway with me in tow this time.

Guess I was an ass no matter what I did.

I shoved open the door with my foot and Lily disappeared inside, presumably right to the bathroom. I had to give it to her, she still remembered the layout to the house. Although, she was right. It had gotten bigger. My dad threw himself into renovating it after my mom passed. He added a third floor that was now set up as a man cave or whatever he called it.

I had only seen it once after he was finished. He decked it out with a bunch of stuff he thought I would love, including another deck with a hot tub and enough lounge chairs that every one of my friends could come over and sunbathe.

After I refused to come up that summer and every proceeding summer the past few years, it must have been covered in a layer of dust.

With Lily still MIA, I made my way to the back of the house where the spare bedrooms were. The split-level house was pretty cool. The entrance was on the second floor with the first floor leading right out onto the dock. Downstairs held the master bedroom and my dad's bar. He would spend most of his time there so Lily and I would be left to the rest of the house.

Footsteps sounded behind me as I pushed open the door at the end of the hall on the left. It was the same bedroom she had always used when visiting, so I figured it would be the most comfortable.

Lily leaned against the doorframe as I tossed her bag onto the bed. A small smile tugged at my lips when I noticed it was the same over-the-top floral comforter my mother picked out all those years ago. I guess my dad couldn't get rid of everything.

"This room hasn't changed," Lily echoed my thoughts as she stepped inside and ran her hand over the bookshelf that housed the many books we read as kids.

"Yeah, looks like my dad didn't change as much as I thought."

"What do you mean? Haven't you been up here the past few summers?"

I cleared my throat and avoided eye contact. It was a secret kept between my dad and me. Whenever he would come up, I would say I was too, but would go camping or on a road trip. Telling everyone that stepping foot inside the house where I spent so much time with my mom was akin to taking a knife to the heart wasn't the type of information I doled out. It wouldn't have made much sense anyway considering we still lived in the house I grew up in. But the lake, it was always something my mom and I shared. Something special about our love for the water.

"Yeah sure," I mumbled, as I made my way out of the bedroom. "I just never come in this room."

"Oh." Lily plopped down on the bed.

I crossed the hall to the bedroom I planned on using. My real bedroom, the one my mom designed for me, was a couple of doors down, the first bedroom in the hall, but I just couldn't.

"Why are you staying in there?" Lily demanded from the hall.

Sometimes I forgot she shared enough of my childhood

to read me. I wasn't used to it, and I certainly didn't like it in this situation.

"Dad never got around to renovating my normal room."

"Uh-huh." She wasn't buying it. Before I could stop her, she raced down the hall and flung open the door. "Looks livable to me. Looks the same, actually."

"Exactly my point." I reached around her, making sure to avert my eyes and slammed the door. "It's a kid's room. Do I look like a kid to you?"

"You look like an ass." She threw a smirk my way and leaned against the closed door. "Seriously, what's your issue with this room? Monsters under the bed? Spider that got away?" Her mouth dropped open as she palmed her chest. "Bad breakup go down in there? Haunted by ghosts of girlfriends past?"

"I just told you, I prefer not to spend all my time in a kid's room. It's kind of a turnoff for the ladies. Who needs a room decorated like the ocean when you have a huge body of water right outside?"

"You're such a bad liar." Lily pushed off the door and poked my chest. "I've seen you get it on in the back of a truck with a bunch of people around and—" She poked my chest again when I opened my mouth to defend myself. "—under the bleachers during a game. Seems to me that the types of girls *you* pick don't have turnoffs."

"Wow, Holladay, seems to *me* that you've been keeping a close eye on my love life." I deflected because I really didn't want to get into it with her. Not with my emotions spiraling.

"I wouldn't exactly call a hookup a love life," she grumbled and smoothed down her hair. "And it's hard not to hear the rumors or, you know, witness it when it's going down at a party I'm attending."

Remember that story for another time? Yeah, not my best moment.

"You make going to a party sound like class. You don't attend a party. You have fun at it. But *fun* is a word you lost a long time ago, isn't it?"

"Whatever, Hayes." She brushed past me and headed for her bedroom. "Let me know when your dad gets here. I need a buffer if you expect to live through the rest of this week."

I smiled at her retreating back. There may have been one small detail I left out when I picked her up. My dad got called into a last-minute project with work. He wouldn't be able to make it until the weekend, which left me exactly four days alone with Lily. Four days to turn her feelings of hate into something that resembled love. Hell, I would even take like.

SIX
Lily

I REMAINED LOCKED in my room for the majority of the afternoon. Parker said his dad would be up by dinner, but after wasting a mindless hour surfing social media, five unanswered texts to Madison, another half hour trying to beat the level I had been stuck on Candy Crush since I quit playing it freshman year, and the thirty minutes I took putting my clothes neatly away... I was pretty much going out of my mind with boredom.

I wasn't lying when I said I needed a buffer. Parker and I hadn't spent more than a few minutes together since we were thirteen. After the car ride, I could almost feel a shift as if we were friends again. He even let me choose the radio station and didn't complain once about my singing along with every song.

But this was Parker. New Parker, not the one I had grown up with. That guy hightailed it out of town around the same time my dad did. In fact, everything changed for both of us the summer before eighth grade, when my dad left, and his mother unexpectedly died. He retreated into a shell, and when he emerged in the fall, he looked like my Parker, but his personality had done a 180. Body-snatchers scary.

But I did have him to thank for Madison. If he hadn't

ditched me to go be Mr. Popular, we never would have become friends. And although I was still kind of pissed at her, I loved her like a sister.

Around five-thirty I couldn't take it anymore. I poked my head out into the hall. Parker's door was closed, and the house was dead quiet. Maybe he was out riding the Jet Skis. I shut my door and grabbed my suit. My mom made good on her promise of buying me a new one. Suit shopping with my mom wasn't my favorite pastime, but I used it as one of the many excuses to stay out of the house to avoid Parker. It was surprising how long you could drag out a simple trip to the mall when desperate.

I slipped on the flimsy material. I had always been a one-piece kind of girl, so I was stunned when my mom bought it for me. Of course, she insisted on buying me the matching cover-up, but whatever. I figured if I had to spend a week at the lake, I might be able to meet a guy. If I did, then it would give me plenty of time to avoid Parker. Simple plan all hinging on my ability, or lack thereof, to flirt.

As I piled my hair up into a messy bun, I did a once-over. Maybe the bikini was a bad idea after all. It was more Madison's style. The lady at the store called it bandage or something. The light-pink bottoms had a bunch of bands on the hips instead of the normal ties. That was all fine and good and I figured they would stay on better out in the water. The top on the other hand...I really don't know what got into me. The color matched the bottoms, and it was considered full coverage, but that was only because it covered the parts of the cup that normally wouldn't be there with a sheer material. On top of the sheer material was a solid delicate flower. It concealed all the important parts, but still left way too much to the imagination. Notably side- and under-boob.

At least there weren't any ties that could get snagged. That happened to Madison once on a school trip to the water park. She almost flashed half of the sophomore class and a crap ton of little kids running around.

I let out a low breath and pulled on the cover-up. I made my choice and I would have to live with it. Parker would just have to keep his eyes to himself. Not that I worried about him ogling me. More like informing me about how inadequate I was compared to his many, many hookups.

A girl's ego could only take so much.

The clock read close to six as I made my way into the kitchen. Still no Parker or Mr. Hayes. Then again, traffic was probably terrible leaving the city on a Tuesday.

I snagged a water bottle from the fridge and surveyed the living room. Parker wasn't kidding when he said his dad renovated. It looked nothing like the lived-in room of my childhood. In place of the comfy worn-in couch sat a modern, brown sectional that I imagined was better to look at than to sit in. All the family photos were gone, replaced with a gigantic white screen. I looked up and saw a projector mounted onto the ceiling.

Fancy.

The staircase to the left was also new. I thought the house looked bigger. I couldn't remember there ever being a third floor. Uncharted territory. With my curiosity taking over, I made my way upstairs. It was ridiculous to feel like some kind of intruder in a house I spent so much time in, but that didn't stop me from flinching with every creak of the wood.

Once I reached the top, I had to do a double take. It wasn't what I expected. In fact, it didn't look like it belonged to the same house. Another one of those huge screens hung on the far wall, damn near taking up the whole thing. The opposing wall had a long, leather couch that looked brand-new. To the left sat a pool table and a minibar, much smaller than the one on the first floor. And to the right, there was a wall made of glass. From the looks of it, it led out onto a deck.

And that moment I realized where I would spend most of my time. Parker wasn't kidding, I did need some color. My skin tone could have rivaled a ghost after the craptastic winter we just came out of. Being from the Pacific Northwest, we live through months of rain, rain, and more rain, leaving most of us sun starved.

I slid open the door and took a deep breath. The house always had a beautiful view. It sat on the lake, for crying out loud. But the new height gave the advantage of seeing the whole lake and Olympic mountains. *Breathtaking* hardly covered it. There was a reason I always loved going there during the summer.

I was so taken with the view I didn't notice the person lounging in a chair until he spoke up and scared the ever-living crap out of me.

Did I mention that attention to my surroundings wasn't a strong trait of mine?

"Gorgeous, huh?" Parker slid his sunglasses to the tip of his nose and peered over them at me.

I tried to answer, I did, but all that came out was a weird gurgling noise. I blamed it on the scare, but it might have had a tiny bit to do with the fact that Parker was topless. Again. And let's just say that chest wasn't the same bony, concave, prepubescent chest I remembered. Somewhere along the way, Parker had filled out. And then some. I had managed to overlook that at the party. Probably because I was doing my best to ignore him in general.

Parker smirked and put his sunglasses back in place. My

whole body flushed red from embarrassment. He one hundred percent caught me ogling him. Parker. A boy I hated. But I couldn't deny those muscles.

He stretched, resting an arm behind his head, and when my gaze dipped taking in the six-pack rippling in the sunlight, I had to look away. Maybe burn my eyes. A lobotomy wouldn't hurt.

Pull it together, Lily.

I plopped down on a lounge chair a couple over from him. Space was definitely welcome. Needed even. With him on the outskirts of my peripheral vision, I could pretend he didn't exist. Get some sun and wait it out until Mr. Hayes arrived.

Only that's not what happened, because the second I got comfortable it was as if someone had injected him with pure caffeine and he wouldn't shut up.

"Need anything to drink?"

I held up my water bottle. Eyes averted.

"Bring sunscreen? I have some if you need it."

"No, thanks."

"No, I don't suppose you would with that sack you're wearing."

"It's a cover-up." Okay, it wasn't the most attractive thing, but my mom insisted. I had never agreed with her fashion choices until that moment.

"It's almost one hundred degrees, why would you want to put more clothes on?"

Because there is no way in hell you need to see what's going on under it—not with everything you got going on over there.

"We can take the Jet Skis out tomorrow if you want," Parker continued before I had a chance to answer his previous question.

"Sure."

"Maybe one of these nights we can go into town. I hear they still have that old-timey ice cream parlor that we used to go to."

"Cool."

Shut up. Shut up. Shut up.

He reminded me of that girl on *How I Met Your Mother* who wouldn't stop talking, to the point where no one could get a word in edgewise.

Don't judge me. My mom loved that show. I had seen the whole series at least three times.

"What do you want for dinner?"

"Whatever your dad is making." I took a long drink of water. Parker wasn't kidding, it was blazing hot out, but I wasn't about to take off the cover-up. Nope. I might even swim in the damn thing. Die in it. Marry it and have little cover-up babies. Presumably not in that order.

"Oh, yeah, about that. Dad texted me earlier. He won't be able to make it until Saturday."

The cool water took a detour down my windpipe, and I bolted upright coughing.

"You okay?" Parker dropped down next to me and patted his hand against my back. I made a feeble attempt to push him off the chair. But he didn't budge. I did, however, notice how hard his chest was.

"What...do...you...mean?" I got out between coughing fits.

"Exactly what I said." He ran a gentle hand down my back as my lungs settled. An involuntary shiver ran through me when his palm met with my bare skin on my lower back where one of the cover-up ties came loose.

If he noticed, he didn't say anything. "Guess something came up. But he Venmoed me money and said to stock up on whatever we want. Which is surprising for him considering—"

"Take me home," I blurted out. I couldn't be there alone with him.

"What?" He settled back in the chair, hands in his lap.

"Take me home. I only agreed to this because my mom thought I would be spending time with you *and* your dad. I'm not hanging out with just you all week. We can't even stand each other."

"That's not true." The tone of his voice almost had me. It sounded hurt. But that wasn't possible. All I spoke was the truth. He couldn't be offended by that.

"Whatever, Parker. Take me home."

"No." The little muscle on the side of his jaw flexed as he looked away.

"Excuse me?"

"I didn't drive all the way up here just to turn around. It would be a complete waste of my week. Besides, if I go home, Dad will just force me into my grueling swimming schedule, and I would prefer a week off."

"Fine." I stood up and made my way to the door. "I'll just call an Uber."

Parker caught my wrist and spun me to face him. "Don't be ridiculous, that would cost hundreds of dollars. You got that laying around?"

I pursed my lips, and he nodded.

"I thought so. Dad will be up here in a few days. In the meantime, we have the lake house to ourselves. I can't think of a better way to start the summer."

Uh, I could think of at least one hundred other ways to start my summer and at least ninety-eight didn't include Parker. Two included burying him somewhere in the desert.

"Swear you didn't do this on purpose." I pulled free of his grasp.

Parker held out his pinkie, and I smiled. I hadn't done a good pinkie swear in forever. I locked mine around his and squeezed, twisting his hand to a weird angle.

"Ow. What the—?"

"If I find out you did this on purpose in some sick play to get me alone, I'll castrate you in your sleep."

With that, I left him standing alone on the deck to enjoy the view that was no longer appealing to me.

Four days. I just needed to get through four days without murdering him.

SEVEN

Lily

I PUSHED the squeaky cart down the crowded aisle, cursing the stupid, wobbly wheel, as Parker walked ahead, scanning the aisles for the particular brand of potato chips he claimed he had been fantasizing about. I offer no judgments about his fantasies. Apparently, his dad wouldn't let him indulge in junk food, which explained his smoking-hot body—something I couldn't deny even though I wanted to. But it didn't explain why Mr. Hayes thought two teenagers would follow his rules when he sent more than $200 without giving us specific instructions.

I had half a mind to force Parker into the same strict dietary regimen that he'd griped about during the entire drive to the store, for kicks. But that would mean I'd have to follow the diet too, and steamed broccoli and skinless chicken breast didn't sound too appetizing. Especially since I lived off coffee and boxed dinners. Geez , my system might go into shock.

I took several minutes, as Parker rambled on, debating the pros and cons of going into shock, but decided an actual sickness wasn't worth the trouble. By that time, we'd reached the store.

What I should have done was stay at the house and left

the shopping to Parker, to give me some peace and quiet. But I was going stir-crazy, and he promised that I could pick out whatever junk food I wanted.

Win-win.

It would have been a triple win if Parker wasn't there at all. But alas, no such luck.

He sauntered over to the beat of the cheery, pop song playing from the overhead speakers, carrying two bags of chips. He held one out. We both laughed.

"Dill pickle?" I snagged the bag from his outstretched hand. "God, we used to cram as many of these as possible in our sandwiches."

"Even in our peanut butter and jelly."

"My mom used to call us monsters." I tossed the bag in the cart. Definitely getting them.

"They just didn't have refined palates like us." He clasped his hands together in front of his chest and scanned the aisle again.

"I think we're stocked plenty. Why don't we get some stuff to make dinner? As much as I love junk food, I don't want to die of a salt-and-sugar coma."

"Ugh, fine." Parker tossed his head back in mock exasperation, the hair on his neck brushing his collar. Much longer than he wore it as a kid. "But I'm getting a ton of pop."

"Sure. Whatever. Go grab that and meet me by the deli. I'm sure I can grill us some steak or burgers."

"Five minutes." Parker held up one hand, fingers spread.

"Three. If I give you that long, you'll get every flavor the store has." He winked at me and walked away.

I headed toward the deli with a strange feeling in my

gut. Almost as if I had swallowed a bag of rocks then topped it off with a gallon of water, leaving my stomach a cramping, gurgling mess. Parker hadn't been the same since the party, and his unusual behavior weakened my resolve to hate him. Sure, he was still a giant jackhole, but we had been so close at one point. Best friends. Inseparable. There might even have been a moment where I thought maybe we would end up together.

Okay, it was more than a moment. Fifth through seventh to be exact. Then he went and ruined it. Shattering my heart in the process. But something about being with him, hanging out just the two of us, brought old feelings to the surface. And those feelings deserved to stay buried, deep, deep down. The last thing I needed was for Parker to figure it out. He would be like a dog with a bone.

"Lily? Lily Holladay?"

I turned toward the masculine voice and almost tipped over my cart. "Milo Moretti?"

The stranger smiled at me and suddenly he wasn't a stranger. Milo was my first boyfriend in middle school, right after the whole Parker-ditching-me thing. We dated for half the year before his parents relocated. Military kid.

He wasted no time scooping me up into a bear hug. My legs dangled off the floor and I couldn't help but notice how tall he had gotten. And muscular. He'd done some growing up in four years.

When he set me down, I was flushed and breathless.

"What are the odds of running into you?" His expression seemed genuine. Friendly. My heart did a little dance in response.

"Like slim to none." I pushed a few strands of hair that his enthusiastic hug had knocked loose, out of my face.

"What are you doing back in Washington? I thought your family moved to California."

"I'm visiting friends. They come every year, and I try to join them when I can. What are you doing up here?"

"Spending a week on the lake."

"No way. Well, it looks like my summer got even brighter." He smiled down at me, revealing that dimple that sucked my thirteen-year-old heart in. It looked even better on his now-scruffy face.

My cheeks warmed as butterflies danced in my stomach to the same rhythm they had whenever Milo used to look at me. Time and distance hadn't killed my first crush. Okay, okay, second crush, but first where something came of it. Embarrassed at the thought that I was being transparent, I glanced away in time to see Parker rounding the corner.

"So, I got cherry, vanilla, and for fun—" Parker stopped dead in his tracks when he took in Milo standing close to me.

Milo turned when he caught my gaze. "Parker? Well damn, it is a small world after all." He extended his hand, but Parker just looked at it, back up to his face, and shrugged motioning with his chin to the three cases of pop in his hands.

"Oh. I'm such a spaz." Milo reached out and took one of the cases from Parker. He sent a wink my way as he leaned over to put it in the cart. "Who you shopping for, a group of ten year olds?"

I chuckled because it was an accurate description of our cart. And Parker. Parker on the other hand, snorted and settled an arm over my shoulders, drawing me to his side. Warmth from his body leached into mine. Spicy cologne invaded my nostrils. A sharp zing shot through my chest.

All of that should have made me angry, murderous, but that's not what happened.

My brain stopped working, grinding right to a halt, and I was pretty sure my lungs were on the way to joining it when Milo glanced at Parker's arm.

"Lily and I figured we would let loose this weekend since we have the lake house to ourselves. Fully stocked bar. Hot tub. Why not add some junk food to the mix?"

My whole body blazed with the sudden rush of blood and heat. What the hell was Parker doing?

"Oh, wow, your parents are cool with you staying up here alone?" A crease formed between his brows as his gaze bounced between us, flicking so fast I was surprised he didn't get dizzy.

"Why not? We've known each other since grade school." Parker leaned his head against mine.

Milo nodded and locked on to me, eyebrows arched.

You can work anytime now, brain. Tell him that Parker is just being an ass—that our parents would have never said yes if the original plan included us alone.

I opened my mouth and...nothing.

Awesome.

"Cool. Cool. Well, I should get back to my friends, make sure they didn't ditch me. Good seeing you, Parker, Lily. Maybe we'll catch each other on the beach..." With that, he left. Ran, actually.

Parker snickered at my side and all at once my brain unlocked. A little too late.

"What the hell, Parker?" I shoved him off me, which only made him laugh harder. Doubled over, clutching his stomach as if it was the funniest thing in the world. In reality, it was the furthest thing from funny. For several reasons. One of which I didn't want to process.

"Oh, come on. It was too good to pass on. You should have seen his face." Parker motioned to where Milo disappeared around the baking aisle. "Besides, Milo is a douche."

"That's funny, I was just thinking the same thing about you." My heart raced from anger. Yeah, anger. It had to be that.

Parker turned to me, all trace of mirth gone. "What, you're telling me you wanted to talk with him? Didn't you two date or something? I saved you."

Saved me? Good lord, the boy had a God complex.

"Yeah, we did, but we ended on good terms. He moved away."

Parker shrugged and grabbed the cart, elbowing me out of the way. "Thought I was doing you a favor. My bad." He left me standing there, fuming, staring at his back.

If he thought he could get away with acting like that, he was sorely mistaken. Suddenly, I couldn't wait to catch him talking to a girl. If he could dish it, then I would make sure he could take it.

⟋

By the time we made it back to the house and unloaded the groceries, all I wanted to do was curl up in bed and read. Parker had other plans.

I winced as he turned up the speakers. The neighbors no doubt could hear every lyric the singer was screaming. Yes, screaming. No idea when or why, but it seemed Parker got into screamo music. And they were bands I hadn't heard since middle school when we both used to make fun of them.

"Mind turning it down?" I yelled, as Parker racked the pool balls.

He ignored me. Or didn't hear me. My ears were bleeding so his had to have been.

I should have gone downstairs and thrown on my headphones, but the speakers were directly above my bedroom. Nothing short of losing my hearing would block it out. So, I set about searching for the remote that controlled the speakers. If I couldn't find it, I wasn't above finding and stealing the power cord.

Right as I started tossing couch cushions aside, a hand landed on my shoulder, followed by hot breath on my ear. "What are you doing?"

I jumped about a foot, whirling around to face an amused Parker. My skin tingled where his mouth had been seconds before. "Turn it down!"

He cupped his hand to his ear, but damn it, I knew he heard me. I shot him my patented death glare, but he just rolled his eyes and walked over to the pool table.

I was going to take that pool cue and shove it up his— The music cut off and Parker waved the remote in the air.

"Happy?"

"Yes, thank you." I headed for the door, but each step I took brought back the music another level. By the time my hand touched the knob, it was blaring again.

"Really?" I yelled.

The screaming halted yet again. Parker cocked his head at me, a stupid grin pulling at his lips. Daring me to try him. The boy was far more obnoxious than I remembered.

"So, you plan to hold me hostage via terrible music?"

"Play pool with me."

"No thanks, I'd rather drink bleach."

The god-awful music started up again, and I groaned, head back, eyes, rolling so he would know how annoyed I was. "One game!" I held up my pointer finger as emphasis.

Parker settled on a reasonable volume before poking me in the ribs with a pool cue. I snatched it out of his hand and shot him another dirty look.

"You break." He stepped out of the way, but I shook my head.

"No way. I haven't played pool in years. You'll be lucky if I don't launch one of the balls off the table and destroy something."

"You were always terrible at it." He lined up his shot, the muscles I shouldn't be noticing in his forearm flexed, and a loud *crack* echoed through the room a few seconds later.

"I wasn't *terrible*." Okay, I totally was, but I wouldn't give him the satisfaction of admitting that.

Several of the balls rolled into the pockets, leaving Parker with his pick.

"You have absolutely no hand-eye coordination. Stripes." Parker bent down and sent another ball straight into the corner pocket next to my hip.

"I had pretty good hand-eye coordination when I punched Mickey Lewis in the throat."

Parker laughed, causing him to miss his shot.

I brushed past him as I tried to determine the best outcome. I didn't have many choices that wouldn't make me look like an uncoordinated idiot. The boy was right. I was terrible at pool. Mini golf. Anything, really, that required me to put a ball into a hole.

"What did he do again to deserve that kind of punishment?"

"He grabbed my ass during Friday assembly." I missed my shot by a mile, and cursed under my breath.

"Oh, that's right. You ended up with detention for a week, and Principal Hudson told him to never sit next to you again." Parker walked behind me, his forearm brushing against mine. For some reason my heart kicked up a notch. He didn't seem fazed.

I cleared my throat, hoping it would calm my heart. "He should have been expelled."

Parker missed his shot.

"If I had been there, he would have gotten more than a punch to the throat."

I managed to sink ten blue. For some reason, I couldn't contain my squeal of excitement. Proving him wrong. "Oh, because little old me can't protect herself?"

"No, because seeing his hands on you would have sent me into a fit of rage." His hazel eyes locked on mine. They had more green in them than I'd remembered.

The pool stick slipped right past the cue ball and slammed into the edge of the table.

I didn't know what to say to that comment, it was so out of left field even in reference to young Parker. Thankfully I didn't need to say anything, and Parker broke the weird vibe with a deep rumbling laugh, and a slap to my upper back. I might have felt that laugh deep in my stomach. And another part of my body.

Get it together, Lily.

"Yeah, you're not terrible at all." Parker's cocky grin was back, helping to reel in my wayward thoughts.

See. It was just Parker. *Parker*. The same boy who filled my umbrella with confetti sophomore year. Let me just say, *wet* confetti is way worse than *dry* confetti. Pretty sure I was still finding it places a year later.

"You distracted me." I pretended to pout, trying my best to keep us on neutral territory. One slip and he would see he was getting to me.

"Uh-huh." Parker sank three shots in rapid succession, leaving him with just the eight ball.

"So..." He leaned up against the bar, cue stick clutched against his chest. His face serious. "You planning on meeting up with Milo?"

Okay, not what I expected him to say.

"That's really none of your business."

"Didn't you guys date all of eighth grade?"

It was surprising Parker even remembered that. We dated the same year Parker ditched me to hang out with the cooler crowd. "Half. He moved in the spring."

"So what, was he like your first kiss or something?" I might have imagined it, but I could have sworn there was an edge to his voice.

"What difference does it make?"

He shrugged. "Just trying to figure out if you're still low-key in love with him or something. Aren't you supposed to be eternally in love with your first kiss?"

"I think you mean the first person you sleep with."

Parker leaned over the table, cue stick gripped so tight in his hand that his knuckles turned white. "So, who's that lucky guy?" He looked up at me, evidently waiting for my answer.

An answer he would have to continue waiting for. "That's none of your business."

Parker took his shot, landing the eight ball in the far-corner pocket.

"Game, I guess. Good job." I tossed the pool stick on the table and headed for the door. I couldn't get down the stairs fast enough.

In the past week I had gone from being harassed by Parker to his forced girlfriend. Then he miraculously let me out of the stupid dare and had been treating me like the friend I once was to him. But the personal questions, digging into my relationships, and blocking Milo from talking to me at the store? That was just plain weird. If I had stumbled into an alternate reality, I wanted back and fast, before my heart got attached again.

EIGHT
Parker

I COULDN'T WAIT for Lily to get up. After getting a whole five hours of sleep, I found myself in the kitchen peering into the fridge, trying to figure out what I could make for breakfast that I wouldn't burn.

Thoughts of Lily ran rampant in my head all night. Which might have had something to do with Milo popping back into her life at the store. Until that point, it almost seemed like we were headed in the right direction. She was talking and most of what she said had nothing to do with murdering me. But then Milo showed up, and I ruined everything by getting possessive.

So, sue me...I had her to myself for a whole week, and I didn't plan on letting another guy swoop in and take that precious time away. Not when I needed every second possible to convince her that I wasn't the grade-A asshat she thought I was.

And if Milo's sudden appearance wasn't bad enough, I let my mouth run away, asking questions I didn't want the answers to. It stung when she confirmed Milo was her first kiss by dodging the question altogether. Whether she liked it or not, I knew her and all of her tells. Avoidance being a biggie. Not like it mattered. I had assumed anyway with the way they were always all over each other. But then she wouldn't answer my question about who the lucky bastard was that stole her V card. Not that I wanted to know. Okay, I totally did, but I shouldn't. There would be no stopping me from hunting the guy down and beating the crap out of him off jealousy alone.

And yes, I was being a complete hypocrite considering I had my share of hookups. Most of which weren't even girl-friends.

I leaned my head against the open refrigerator door. Focus. I needed to focus. Screw Milo. Screw every other guy she'd been with. Those were repercussions I would have to live with. After all, there wouldn't have been any other guys if I hadn't ditched her. I would have made sure of it.

Food. Focus on food.

I grabbed the milk out of the fridge and set it next to the fancy coffee machine my dad bought earlier in the year. Something about it steaming milk and whatever else baristas at coffee shops did. I had a little time to figure it out before Lily woke up. From what I remembered of her prac-tically falling out of her front door most school days, the girl wasn't a morning person.

I glanced at the clock. Almost eight. I could figure out the coffee then maybe she would help me with breakfast. We had bought eggs and bacon, which, with my cooking skills, would end up a burnt mess. Not all that impressive when your main goal is to *impress* someone.

Right as my hand brushed against the instruction manual for the machine, Lily appeared in the kitchen.

"And here I thought I could have a few hours without you this morning." The sass was strong in her tone, leading me to believe she slept about as much as I did. I could only hope it was due to her thinking about me in a non-murderous way for once.

She stretched, seemingly unbothered by me. Sleeping made her hair a disheveled mess, sticking up on one side in a cute little bird's nest. She tugged at the hem of her shirt, one that was at least two sizes too big, fanning it as if she wished I hadn't caught her wearing it. I'd seen her in worse. Her favorite Mickey Mouse onesie came to mind. I was about to voice that when my gaze drifted down, and I caught sight of nothing but legs. If she had on shorts, they were tiny enough to qualify as underwear.

I knew her legs were long. After all, she was taller than most guys our age. But the way the shirt fell, hitting just below the crest of her butt made them look even longer.

"You should take a picture. It will last longer."

Her voice snapped me out of whatever creepy stare I had fallen into. I caught her smirk as she made her way to the refrigerator. Alert and already on the attack. The odds were most definitely not in my favor. Not without the voodoo magic of coffee.

"I think I fried my brain trying to figure out this coffee machine." I held up the manual as if it was at all believable. The damn thing still had the plastic wrap on it.

"Oh my God, you do *not* have one of these. Aren't they like two grand?" She leaned around me, taking in the fancy beast occupying half the counter space.

"How should I know? My dad bought it." I tore off the plastic wrap and flipped through the pages. "Apparently, we can make store-quality coffee or something. But this might as well be in Chinese." I turned the book upside down and tilted my head for emphasis.

Lily giggled and snatched it out of my hand. "So helpless."

"Just wait until you see me try to cook." I reached into the refrigerator and pulled out the eggs and bacon.

Her face fell as she clutched the manual to her chest. "Please tell me you're not going to attempt bacon. Didn't you almost burn down the house last time?"

"I was nine." I grabbed a cast-iron pan from the open shelves above the stove. "And you were the one who demanded I make it."

"It would have gone perfect with our maple-pecan ice cream." She pried the carton of eggs out of my hands as I went to open it. "As much as I love seeing you struggle. Boy, do I *love* seeing you struggle." She hip-checked me. "I would prefer not to burn down your dad's house. Looks like he spent your entire life savings renovating."

She was close to the mark, actually. I would be lucky if we had enough for college. Which is why Dad pushed swimming so hard. He felt bad about spending all our money, and I felt bad bringing it up since I figured it was part of his grieving process. A scholarship was my only option. Just another reason swimming no longer appealed to me.

"How about I figure out the coffee machine—or worst-case scenario, go buy some—and you do breakfast?"

She let out an exasperated noise. "Fine. But don't get used to it. I expect you to live off cereal for the next three days."

Lily got to work making breakfast, starting with the bacon, and I realized I would have done it backward leaving the eggs ice-cold by the time the bacon finished.

The sizzling was a welcoming sound. The last time bacon was made in my house was when my mom was still alive. Dad and I were pretty much helpless in the kitchen if it wasn't premade or cooked on the grill.

Lily hummed under her breath, swiping hair out of her face with the back of her hand. I tried to focus on the coffee, but I caught myself wondering if her hair was as soft as it used to be. It was a lot longer than she kept it when we were kids, that's for sure. And even in its messy, bed-head state, it maintained her signature waves. Somewhere between curly and not. Synonymous with Lily.

"You know, I'm starting to think you have a staring problem." Lily side-eyed me as she flipped over the bacon.

Shit. I was staring, wasn't I?

"Just dreaming about that bacon."

Yeah, sure, that was believable.

Lily snorted, giving me the impression she felt the same exact way. What was wrong with my brain? No other girl, ever, flustered me enough to act like a total creep.

I put my eyes back where they belonged on the coffee machine and fought the urge to steal another glance. She was still wearing those itty-bitty shorts, after all.

"I think I figured it out," I called, seven long minutes later, after forcing myself to concentrate. I poured milk into the pitcher and set the steam wand inside. While it heated, I pressed the button for the espresso.

With my luck, I'd burn that too.

"Good, 'cause breakfast is almost ready." Lily took the plate of bacon out of the microwave and placed it on the island before transferring the scrambled eggs to each of our plates. "This kitchen is amazing."

You're amazing.

I winced and shoved the thought out of my head. I would never win her over by creeping her out. And the fact that even I thought it sounded pathetic gave me the impression she would be more than creeped out. Or turned off.

I slid the cup of coffee in front of her as she settled onto one of the barstools. She eyed it suspiciously before she wrapped her hand around the handle and brought it to her lips. I held my breath. It was the fanciest coffee I had ever attempted. My experience before this had been pouring whatever my dad brewed into a cup and topping it with milk.

"Wow." She wiped her wrist across her lips, removing the tiny bit of foam that settled there. "Color m impressed."

I couldn't stop the stupid grin that took over my face. Impressed was far better than annoyed.

Lily grabbed a substantial helping of bacon before pushing the plate in my direction. One thing I loved most in a girl was if she wasn't afraid to eat. For some reason I assumed Lily would have grown out of that. Evidently, she could still eat me under the table.

I took a bite of the scrambled eggs and moaned. Seriously, it had been way too long since I had them. And I didn't count IHOP. Rumor had it, they put pancake mix into their eggs. My father put a quick end to our trips there when he found out. Extra carbs during the season were strictly forbidden.

"Good?" Lily nibbled on a piece of bacon, turning her attention to the window overlooking the lake, her expression full of longing.

"Want to take the Jet Skis out?"

"Nah." After a gulp of her coffee she turned to me. "Figured I would go down to the beach and just relax. Bring a book or something."

"I could be into that. Well, you know, without the whole reading thing."

"We really don't have to spend *every* second together. You do your thing. I'll do mine, and we'll get through this week without killing each other. Then we'll have the rest of the summer, and we can go on pretending the other one doesn't exist. Everything will be right with the world again."

My stomach sank. The progress I had thought we made proved to be nothing more than wishful thinking. Suddenly, I couldn't control the urge to piss her off. Most of the time I did it just to get her attention, but in that moment, all I wanted to do was make her feel as irritated as I was.

"Whatever, 4.0. Have fun nerding out all by yourself. I'll be out having fun on the water. Maybe I'll even swing by Tracy McHugh's house. I heard she's up here for the summer, and her parents gave her an early graduation present that I've been dying to get my *hands* on."

Lily's face fell. "You're a pig."

I dumped the remaining bacon onto her plate. "And you eat like one. No wonder you haven't had a boyfriend since eighth grade. No guy likes girls who can out eat them. You should take a few pointers from Madison. Then again, why compete with her when you know you'll lose?"

Lily's mouth dropped open as her face flushed a shade of red I hadn't quite seen before. If the fire in her eyes was anything to go by, she had murder—specifically mine—on her mind.

I left her sitting there to eat or stew or clean up, and stalked off to my room to change. In the time it took to walk down the hall and slam my door, the reality of my comments set in.

I had essentially called her fat. Insinuated that her best friend was more attractive than her, which was a bald-faced lie. And threw my own promiscuous behavior in her face.

Because nothing makes a girl swoon for you like the Douchebag Trifecta.

An hour later, I sat in the middle of the lake, drifting in the waves the few boats on the water created. I never thought I could be sad on a Jet Ski, but there I was, sulking. After my comments, there was no way in hell I would be able to get back into Lily's good graces. In fact, she would probably try to poison me the next chance she got. Which meant I was also on my own for lunch. And dinner. Then right back around to breakfast until my dad came up.

I glared at the beach not far off in the distance. It was crowded for being early. I tried to pick out Lily's form, but it was useless.

My only options were to go home and see if she was there, or go find her on the beach. There was a possibility she wouldn't make a scene at the beach. Slim, but much better than my chances of catching her at home.

With groveling in mind, I swung by the dock and tied up the Jet Ski before walking down to the beach. Much as I expected, bodies littered the shore. Someone had set up a volleyball net and a rowdy game of boys versus girls looked to be coming to an end. Girls lay out on their towels, most with bikinis that had to have been classified as lingerie. Not that I was complaining. But if Lily were there, she must be as uncomfortable as she looked in Madison's skirt.

Which might actually work in your favor.

My eyes swept the shore, searching for one person who seemed out of place. Problem was, no one stood out. Not a single fidgeting girl in a one-piece bathing suit that had to have been a few years too old. Okay, so I might have seen her at the community pool a few times. And there might have been a high chance I was there just to see her since I didn't make a habit of swimming off-season.

Right as I was about to turn and head back to the house

to make sure she hadn't called an Uber to take her home, I heard a familiar giggle.

It took me only two seconds to zero in on the source. Ice filled my veins, then was immediately replaced with a rush of heat when I saw Milo standing over Lily—who had changed into that ugly, dress thing—shaking his wet hair at her as she tried to hide beneath her towel. A large umbrella cast a shadow over her, tilting with the slight breeze, which explained why I had missed her the first time.

I attempted to uncurl my hands from tight fists, but the closer I got and the more I could plainly hear the flirting, blinding jealousy took over.

Why couldn't she be that carefree with me? Milo had dumped her when he moved away and that she forgave. My mom died, and I needed space, and for that she chose to hold a grudge.

Lily whipped her towel at Milo who dodged with ease, giving the end a playful tug. Neither one of them saw me, and for a fleeting second, the rational part of my brain told me to cut my losses and go home. The other side told me to break it up before she invited him back. Because if she did that, I would be tempted to break his jaw. Doing that would shatter my hopes of getting a swimming scholarship.

"Fancy you guys running into each other. *Again.*" Milo looked over at me, shielding his eyes from the sun right as the smile dropped from Lily's face.

My gut twisted when I realized I was the one who took that away from her. The disapproving glare she sent my way was all me.

I should have gone back to the house.

"Hey, Parker," Milo called, his stupid, friendly demeanor sending me right back into irritation.

"Tracy's gifts turn out to be less appealing than you

thought?" Try as she might, Lily couldn't hide the sharpness of her tone.

So, she was still pissed.

"Figured I would save them for a special occasion." Tracy was the furthest thing from my mind. Something I should have told her then and there. Instead, my guard went up.

Lily snorted. "Like the next time you're at a crowded party?"

Milo glanced between us, smart enough to read that something was going on, and took a step backward. "Well...I should probably get back to my friends."

"Don't be silly. Parker is just leaving." She shot me another glare and mouthed the word *bye* at me.

"Parker isn't, actually." I surveyed the surrounding area, noticing quite a few girls from our class. "Besides, what kind of boyfriend would I be if I let my girl sit here all by herself? It might give guys the wrong impression." I locked eyes with Milo, making sure he heard me.

"You're *not* my boyfriend." Lily jumped up and turned toward Milo, arms waving between them. "He's not my boyfriend."

I almost lost it then and there when I saw the look on Milo's face. Okay, yes, it was a dick move, butting in between two people who clearly had a flirt session going on. It was even worse that I went back on my agreement to let the whole dating dare go. But no way in hell would I be able to survive a whole week of them hanging all over each other.

"Well, whatever is going on, I don't wanna get in the middle of. It was good seeing you, Lily." Milo gave her a weak smile before walking off toward his friends.

Lily turned on me, face puckered and back to that

impressive shade of red. "Seriously? What the hell is wrong with you?"

"Nothing, but I sure as hell didn't want that moron hanging around my house for the next week."

Partial truth, but I wasn't about to tell her it was because of jealousy. She wouldn't have believed me anyway.

"Besides, I saved you. *Again*. The dude is a player." I motioned to the shore where Milo was seconds away from plunging into the water with a leggy blonde draped on his shoulder.

"Oh yeah, I forgot... What guy would want me, right?" She scooped up her towel and bag before storming past me.

"Lily, wait."

"Screw you, Parker."

Several faces turned in my direction out of curiosity. We probably were the first fight, but we wouldn't be the last. The lake was notorious for hookups and heartbreak. By the end of the day, the word around would be that Lily and I had some kind of lovers' quarrel. Thankfully, by the next day, everyone will have moved on to someone else.

With a deep breath, I bent over to grab the umbrella Lily left behind. If I hurried, I might catch her before she requested that Uber.

NINE
Lily

My THUMB HOVERED over the order button for the Uber. Sure, with surge pricing it would cost close to two hundred according to the estimate, but it would be money well spent if it meant I could get far away from Parker.

Who the hell did he think he was, anyway? After explicitly promising to let the whole dare go, he used it against me the first chance he got. Twice butting in when Milo and I were reconnecting, all while having plans to test-drive Tracy's new chest. Hypocrite on all levels.

With a groan that came out as a growl, I flopped onto the bed letting my sandals fall to the floor in the process. If I didn't know any better, I would think Parker was jealous. But that didn't make any sense. He made it perfectly clear during breakfast that he saw me as a fat, unattractive girl. One he would never come near unless it was to torture me for an entire summer.

Maybe I could convince my mom to move...

A rattling knock on the door caused me to jump. I scowled at the wood. He had some serious balls to come right to me after acting the way he did. I glanced at my phone. How mad would my mom be if I charged two hundred dollars? If Madison would answer my damn texts, I wouldn't need a car service.

"Lily, can you open up?" The handle shook, but thankfully I had the forethought to lock it.

"Go away."

"Come on. Look...I'm sorry, okay?"

I sat up, gripping my phone hard enough to make my hand ache. Did he just say he was sorry?

"Lily, did you hear me?"

So, he treats me like crap for years and thinks one apology makes up for it? Screw that.

"Go away, Parker. I need to pack. My Uber will be here soon."

"You ordered an Uber?" His voice shot up a couple of octaves, and I had to suppress a giggle. I hadn't called it...yet.

"Cancel it. If you really want to leave, I'll drive you, but can you please hear me out?"

Against my better judgment, I unlocked the door and swung it open. He looked remorseful at least, but it didn't affect my simmering rage. "Well?"

"I'm sorry for the beach. For the store. For everything. I'll go down there and tell Milo right now that I was just messing around if that's what you want."

"Oh yeah, that won't look desperate."

Parker growled, his eyes darkening as they locked on to mine. "What do you want then? I can apologize till I'm blue in the face, but I get the distinct impression that won't make a lick of difference."

What did I want? Well for one, I wanted to travel back in time and not go to that party. That's where the summer went wrong. If I hadn't gone, Madison wouldn't have been able to screw me over, and I would be at home enjoying my Parker-free time. All those thoughts bubbled right to the surface, and when I was seconds away from voicing them, I caught on to the uncomfortableness in Parker's posture. Rolled shoulders. Fidgeting feet. Tic in his jaw. He only did that when he was uneasy.

Could it be he had a conscious after all?

"What I want..." Parker shut his eyes, bracing for my answer. An answer I really wanted to use to rip him a new one. But, I didn't. Couldn't. One-hundred-percent pathetic on my part. "What I want is to have a peaceful week at the lake. And the only way that will happen is if we aren't at each other's throats. So, I propose a truce."

Parker cocked his head, skepticism radiating off him. I didn't blame him. "A truce?"

"For the week. We can go on hating each other when we get back, but for the next week all bad feelings are put to the side and we act civilized. Which means no calling me fat and no more twat-blocking me."

Parker sputtered, his eyes growing wide before he collected himself. "Did you just say 'twat-blocking'?"

"Yes. As in stop butting in where you're not wanted. Do we have a deal?"

"I'm still hung up on the fact that you said 'twat-blocking'."

"Parker!" I threw my hands up in exasperation. "Not the point. The point is that we call a truce. Which includes being nice to each other and not jumping in the middle of flirting or flings or whatever you do when you're alone with a girl."

A girl who was stupid enough to be alone with him is what I wanted to say, but alas it would have gone against my whole truce angle.

"Just this week?" he asked.

"Just a week. Think you can handle that?"

He seemed to mull it over for a few seconds before thrusting his hand out between us. "Deal."

I gripped his hand, ignoring the urge to inflict pain. "Who knows, maybe when you're not being a jackass, you'll attract a nice respectable girl."

Okay, I planned it to be my last low blow. I also planned on him retorting with some smart-ass remark about how he likes his girls less respectable... You know, the only kind he could attract. Instead he gave me a sly smile and pulled me close.

"That's the plan."

His thumb trailed over my skin, sending a zing up my arm. It came out of nowhere, a feeling I hadn't experience since I was younger. Fear laced through my chest and I quickly extracted my hand, praying that my face remained its normal, pale color.

"So, what should we do with the rest of the day?" I asked in an attempt to distract him.

If Parker noticed my uncomfortableness, he didn't let on. "We can go back to the beach. If you want?"

Oh, yeah, and be the main attraction to everyone who witnessed our blowup. No thanks. "Umm, those people who saw us screaming at each other are probably still there. Maybe we can hold off on the beach until tomorrow?"

Parker nodded in agreement. "I was out on the Jet Ski earlier and the water was nice. Not too many boats. Wanna go out?"

I hadn't been on a Jet Ski since I was in middle school. Excitement replaced my unease. "Will you let me drive?"

"Do you have a license?"

Crap. "No."

"Then it looks like you'll just have to tag along with me. Ride bitch, just like you did as a kid."

Parker yanked on the sleeve of my cover-up and dragged me to the stairs. I attempted to push him off me, but he threaded his fingers into the crochet fabric that adorned the edges. Somewhere along the way, I gave in to a fit of giggles. It made no sense how I could go from hating his guts to a giddy child, but the more I thought about the lake, the more images of us as kids popped into my head. We used to have the best time out on the water from sunup until sundown, reluctantly coming in when our parents made us.

Like I said, Parker was interwoven into my entire childhood. The good memories and the bad.

He let me go once we reached the dock. As he bent down to untie the Jet Ski, I noticed that it floated in place of the boat his dad loved almost as much as Mrs. Hayes. Either he sold it to help pay for the renovations or he had it stashed away somewhere. My guess, considering how much it would have reminded him of his wife, he stored it in the gigantic shed off the side of the house.

I leaned sideways, catching a peek before I felt Parker tug on my hand. "Come on, princess. Let's see if you can hold on as good as you used to."

I pinched his shoulders as I settled behind him. "*One* time I fell off. You caught me off guard. You made up some big story about how you saw the Loch Ness Monster, and when I let go to look over the side you took off. Total cheap shot and doesn't count against my perfect score."

"Uh-huh." Parker attached the key to his wrist and turned around so he could see me. "You gonna ride with that cover-up on?" He hauled his shirt over his head then tossed it onto the dock.

Heat radiated off his back, penetrating through to my own skin. Yeah, I wasn't about to wrap around him practically naked. "I might get cold out there."

Parker shrugged and slipped the key into the ignition. The Jet Ski bobbed in the water as he took his foot off the dock, and a few seconds later the roar from the engine blocked out the peaceful sounds of the lake.

I wrapped my arms around his waist, locking my hands around my forearms and noticing that to do so I had to lean a lot closer than I did in the past. My cheek was practically resting on his ripped back. Yes, ripped. Not an area I generally thought about on a guy, but all the swimming had done his muscles good, and for a fleeting second, backs became the number one hottest muscle group on a guy, smacking abs right out of the way. Then I realized who I was thinking about, and I pushed that thought right out, instead focusing on my celebrity crush, Ryan Reynolds. *Hello,* abs.

Parker maneuvered the Jet Ski out of the dock and away from the five-mile zone.

"Ready?" Before I could answer, he punched the gas, whipping me backward and almost throwing me off the back.

I squealed and gripped on to him tighter. I may have been untossable when we were little, but it looked like I was a bit rusty. Parker let out his own cry of excitement and maneuvered to the left, sending both of us sliding as he aligned the tip of the water ski at the rolling waves that a passing boat created.

Without hesitation, he gunned it, lifting up off the seat at the last second. I followed suit, falling into a rhythm. Parker loved the big jumps. He used to say it made it easier to toss me when I wasn't planted on the seat. I don't know where he got that idea from because, as I mentioned earlier, he had only ever thrown me once.

Parker veered to the right, spraying our legs with icy

water as he searched out another set of waves. As he had mentioned, the lake wasn't as busy as I would have expected. Then again, it was early in the summer. Come Fourth of July, the lake would be so packed that there would hardly be any room for the amount of watercrafts on the water.

By the second set of waves, my arms ached from how hard I held on to him. When we were little, our parents forced us to wear life jackets. They had so many straps it was easy to find something to grab on to. Sans life jackets and a shirt, I didn't have much to secure myself to unless I wanted to use his pecs. The thought alone made my face burn. I wiggled in my seat, lowering my arms to the narrower part of his stomach. Unfortunately, doing so brought me closer to him, forcing my chest into his back and squeezing my thighs tighter to the outside of his.

Parker stiffened and, judging by the way his ribs expanded into my forearms, his breathing sped up. The Jet Ski slowed, and Parker turned his head to see me. "Doing okay back there?"

I knew for a fact my face reddened by the way Parker grinned. Stupid body. "Yeah, just trying to find a place to hold on to. It was so much easier as kids with how scrawny you were."

As soon as the words were out of my mouth, I realized how they sounded. Yes, anyone with eyes could see how built Parker had gotten from the many, many hours he spent swimming. But my eyes were not supposed to notice those things about him. And since I had already noticed it three times in two days, I figured the shock of being around him again was making me a tad bit insane.

Parker shook his head, no doubt at my expense. "Wanna do another lap?"

I scooched in a little closer, trying and failing to break our gaze. "Sure."

What was I doing? What I should have said was *no, please take me back to shore so I can recenter my thoughts back on hating you.*

Parker didn't wait for me to change my mind. He accelerated so quickly I lost my grip. My limbs moved of their own free will. My right leg jumped up, stacking my thigh on top of his and tucking my foot under his calf. My hands did exactly what I thought about earlier, and gripped on to his chest muscles, my fingers digging in for dear life. I was pretty sure my whole spider monkey movement caught him off guard because Parker let out a gasp, his fingers loosening on the hand grips.

Two seconds later both of us plunged into the freezing-cold water. Yup, one week into summer wasn't enough to warm the water. It felt like a thousand razor blades sliced through my skin at the exact same time. Almost enough to make me gasp underwater, which would have been bad news for my lungs.

I broke the surface first, sputtering and wiping water droplets out of my eyes. The Jet Ski bobbed in the water not far off. Luckily for us there were no passing boats because without a life jacket and no way to alert them, that could have spelled danger.

Parker bobbed up next to me on a deep inhale. He blinked a few times before locking on me. "Trying to murder me?"

"What?" I laughed and slapped my hand onto the surface of the water sending a spray in his direction. "You're the one who took off like you were being chased. I simply did what I could to remain dry. Taking you with me was just a bonus."

Parker shook his head and ran a hand through his matted hair. "I think that's the first time you managed that."

"Well, considering it was only the second time you sent me off, odds were in my favor."

A boat passed by in the distance, rippling the water. "Come on." Parker thumbed at the driverless ski. "Let's get out of the water before we get killed."

I hung back, taking a moment to admire the effortless way he swam through the water. Water god for sure. I swear he sliced through it like a knife through butter, hardly making a splash.

Parker pulled himself up first and offered me his hand. I had half a mind to yank him in with it, but the chill running through my body made me rethink that. It would just delay us getting back to the dock. Out of breath, I slipped my hand into his. I wanted to blame the warmth that spread up my arm on the sun shining on us. But when he smiled down at me and yanked me up in one fluid motion, the warmth spread to my stomach and I knew I would be lying to myself. Being around Parker alone was dangerous for my heart especially when he was acting like my old friend.

Parker directed the Jet Ski toward the dock, and a few minutes later he backed us in and cut the engine.

Silence fell over us, and since my stupid heart wasn't to be trusted, I said the first thing that popped into my head. "Next time, let's make sure to wear life jackets."

Parker let out a rumbling laugh, tipping his head backward. Water droplets fell from the strands and splattered on my thigh. "Agreed. I forgot how much work it was getting back after being thrown."

He had to have said that for my benefit. Nothing about being in the water was hard for him.

"The water is a lot colder than I remember."

"We used to come up during Fourth of July. By then, it had plenty of time to heat up." Parker set his foot down on the dock and cleared his throat.

That's when I realized I was still holding on to him. I let go like he was on fire and scooted back so he could hop off. Once the Jet Ski had been tied up, I stood and jumped to the dock before he could offer his hand again. I was pretty sure I would need to instate a no-touching rule if I was going to survive the week.

"Up for some lunch?" Park brushed a few water droplets off his shoulder. My eyes tracked the movement, taking in the way his shoulder flexed and the vein in his forearm popped out.

Bad Lily.

"Um, no. I think I'm going to lay out on the deck and dry off. Then maybe take a nap or something. I didn't sleep well last night."

Parker nodded his head looking like maybe he wanted to say something. Instead, he backed up toward the house. "I'm kinda tired too. I'll grab a shower and take a nap as well. We'll meet up for dinner or something."

Parker left me standing on the dock staring after him. Heat from the sun-soaked wood started to burn my feet, but all I could do was think about Parker in the shower.

It would be a miracle if I made it through the week, and this time it wouldn't be because I wanted to kill him.

TEN
Parker

"YOU'RE A DIRTY LITTLE CHEAT!" Lily tipped her cards back as I reached for them, confirming my suspicion.

"You can't cheat at Bullshit because the whole point of the game *is* to cheat."

I shot her a dirty look and picked up the stack of cards that somehow became mine even though I knew for a fact she wasn't holding two sevens.

Lily winked and rearranged her six cards in an over-the-top fashion as I tried to get my twenty in order. After the Jet Skiing the day before, we avoided each other like the plague. Which was fine by me. Both of us stayed in our rooms, and I was fairly certain we both kept an ear out for when the other emerged to grab food because we managed to not cross paths. If I hadn't mistaken the sound of the shower door, we might not have seen each other for the rest of the trip.

Kind of went against the whole winning her over plan, but the spark I felt—the spark I know for a fact she felt—became overwhelming. Especially considering our surroundings.

I had half a mind to hide out until my dad was there as a buffer. With him talking nonstop, there wouldn't be any weird, uncomfortable lulls like there had been when I caught her off guard in the hall. Which is how we ended up sitting around my family's old kitchen table well past sundown playing Bullshit. I had found the deck of cards earlier when, out of pure boredom, I organized the guest room closet. It was the first thing I thought of after bumping into each other. Thankfully, she agreed.

"Have you tried out the Jacuzzi yet?" Lily asked.

"Not yet. Been too hot during the day and I've been keeping my grandpa's sleeping schedule. I don't even go to bed this early during the school year."

Lily laughed and shuffled her cards again. "The sun gets to you after a while. I remember as kids we would pass out five seconds after our heads hit the pillow after spending all day out in the sun."

"Two eights." I tossed down the cards. "Might also have to do with vigorous games of tag and the many hours knee-boarding."

"That too." Lily chuckled. "Three nines."

Flat-out lying again, but I let her have it. The best way to beat someone at Bullshit was to let the stack get big enough where recovery was near impossible.

"Do you remember how your mom would sneak us ice cream even if we'd already had dessert? Your dad would get so mad and go off on one of his healthy food kicks. And how we were—" Lily stopped laughing and her face fell when she realized what she said. "Oh, Parker, I'm sorry. I wasn't thinking. It just came out."

With a shrug, I turned to my cards. It stung talking about her, especially in the house. Like I could feel her. Or what was left of her after Dad gutted the place. But even worse was that I remembered that argument like it was yesterday. The night before my mom died. Every word would forever be etched in stone on my heart because it was the same year that I stopped loving to swim.

"Really, I'm so sorry." Lily dropped her cards and reached for my hand, eyebrows pinching together with genuine concern.

We'd never talked about it. Not once. Lily was there. She watched in horror with me as the ambulance loaded up my mom. She was there for the funeral a few days later. She even tried to be there for me the following weeks before school started up. But my shattered heart just couldn't deal with it. I didn't want to talk about how empty life felt—not with the girl who didn't belong in the darkness. Not with the girl who I considered akin to sunshine. So, I shut her out, figuring that instead of dragging her down, I would let her move on. It wasn't as if she lost a parent.

But then she did.

Her dad walked out on them a week before school started. Try as I might, I couldn't pull myself out of my grief to help with hers. Even though she had tried to be my rock. That summer, childhood ended, and we realized life wasn't always good. Fun didn't last and love certainly didn't.

That's what I tried to tell myself when I saw her in the halls that fall. But as my grief faded and my heart opened back up, Lily's had done the opposite. I was too late.

"You don't have to be sorry." My thumb traced a circle across the edge of her hand. They had gotten softer since we were kids.

"I miss her, too, you know. Being in this house. I feel her."

Tears threatened me. I hadn't cried since her funeral, but for some reason, sitting in the house she died in, talking with the girl I lost, my emotions flared to life all at once, reminding me that I wasn't made of stone and sarcasm.

"Want to check out the hot tub?" Lily offered with a shake of our hands. "I've been eyeballing it since we got here."

Hell yes came to mind. Instead I said, "Why are you being so nice all of a sudden? Don't you hate my guts?"

Lily sat back in the chair, arms crossed. "I don't hate you, Parker." She caught my skeptical look. "Okay, so I have had many, many moments where I loathed you. But no matter how many times I thought I hated you when you would push my buttons and be an all-around jackass, I couldn't. You'll always be a huge part of my life. A lot of happy memories are tied up in you."

Lily took a swig of her pop. "But I'll deny ever saying any of this, so don't get any ideas about telling people."

The sadness gripping my heart lessened, allowing me to return to my normal self. "Man, too bad I have it recorded." I waved my phone and Lily's eyes widened. Total lie, but she didn't know that.

"You do not!" She reached across the table, swiping for the phone, but I jumped up and out of her reach. "I take back everything I said. Parker Hayes is a jackass."

"Not recording anymore, Lil. But now, I'll forever have your love saved on my phone."

"Parker, hand over the phone." Lily skirted around the table and I backed up into the living room. "I'm serious. Madison catches one word of that, and she'll never let it drop."

I took another step backward as she advanced. I'd seen that look many times. She was seconds away from rushing me, much like she had when I would take one of her things just to mess with her. "All of my childhood happiness is because of you," I mocked, in the best girly tone I could muster.

"That is *not* what I said."

"It's what I heard."

"Parker, give me the phone or I swear I'll—"

I dodged her grabbing hand, holding the phone high above my head. "You'll what, Lil?"

She didn't answer. Instead she charged, catching me off balance and knocking me over the arm of the couch. I landed on my back, the air pressing out of my lungs as she landed on top of me. The phone flew across the room, clattering to the ground somewhere past the coffee table.

Lily burst out laughing and rubbed at a red spot on her forehead. "Your chest is made of stone. I think your dad should let you eat a few burgers now and then."

"First you love me, now you're talking about my hot body? What's gotten into you, Holladay?"

"Shut up." Lily smacked my chest. That was it. Neither one of us attempted to move. Even as my palm settled on her lower back and our labored breathing forced our chests together.

Silence stretched between us, and for once, I had no words. All of them gone. Evaporated into nothing when our eyes met. Electricity flowed through my veins, the strange tingling forcing my hand to the side of her face where I tucked a strand of hair behind her ear.

A boat horn blared on the water outside the front window. Tension broke and Lily snapped out of it first.

"So..." Lily cleared her throat and used my chest to push herself up, copping a feel along the way. Not that I minded.

"Want to check out the hot tub now? I mean I've clearly whooped your ass in Bullshit, so no point continuing." She held her hand out to me.

"Just trying to get me topless again, Holladay?" I grabbed on before she could take it back.

"So full of yourself, Hayes." Lily backed up the second I was standing. "But if you don't want to..."

"No," I said a little too quickly. So quickly, in fact, that there was no smooth way to recover. It didn't stop me from trying. "It would make me a sore loser if I couldn't sit out there and take the inevitable gloating from the whooping you gave me and not just in cards. Nice tackle, by the way." I ended the sentence with a soft shoulder punch that left Lily looking confused.

"So...I'll meet you up there?"

"Sure." I ran my fingers through my hair to give myself something to do besides stand there looking like an idiot. "I'll grab us a few pops and meet you up there."

Lily nodded and headed off to her room. The second she was out of sight, I let out a long breath. She had to think I was unstable. There was a possibility I was.

Shaking my head, I headed into the kitchen. Clear my thoughts, that's all I needed to do. We were on the right track. Talking. Laughing. Touching. If I could keep myself centered, then all I had to worry about was aligning her feelings to mine. Easy.

Luckily for me, I already had my swim trunks on. Earlier, before the run-in, I had planned to spend the day lakeside avoiding her and never got around to changing.

I grabbed two Cokes from the fridge and headed up to the deck. On my way outside, I flipped on the radio and used my phone to set up a little less-screamy radio station on Pandora. I settled on a 2000s channel, with songs we used to listen to as kids.

By the time I had the cover off and the bubbles going, Lily joined me, dressed in the hideous shirt-dress-thing.

"So, I have to ask." I pointed to her attire. "Mom pick that out?"

"Pretty much." She grinned, dipping her hand into the water. "Perfect temperature."

I nodded and slipped my shirt off, tossing it on a nearby lounge chair. "Dad must have this serviced in the off-season or something."

"Does he rent the place out? I remember how gorgeous it was up here during Christmas."

"I dunno." The water warmed my muscles as I sank inside. The real reason my dad got it was so I could soak after he killed me out on the lake practicing. When I refused to come up, it pretty much became a waste of money.

Lily stood by the side, chewing on her lip.

"Are you gonna stare or join me?"

Her fingers played with the little dangly strings hanging off the hem of her shirt before nodding and pulling it up over her head.

My heart stopped. My mouth dropped open. And I was fairly certain my eyes bugged out of my head. Lily's cheeks flamed red as she moved to get into the hot tub. I had seen her in a bathing suit before, but always a one-piece, and over the past few years it was from a distance.

The scraps of fabric that clung to her body left little to the imagination, and that's saying something because my imagination could come up with a lot. None of my wayward thoughts over the years added up to the woman who stood in front of me. Four years changed her from a scrawny tomboy into a knock-out, filling out in all the right places. Places she hid behind modest clothing most days. Places I wanted my hands to roam every second of the day.

She sank into the water with a moan, cutting off my train of thought and the view of those flirty flowers covering the most intimate part of her chest. I could feel her staring at me, and I had to will myself to meet her gaze.

The first words in my head flew right out. "So... I'm assuming your mom didn't pick out the bikini?"

Stupid. Stupid. Stupid.

I closed my eyes and sank lower into the water wishing to disappear completely.

Lily chuckled and reached for her pop. "No. I'm actually surprised she got it, honestly. Maybe she was hoping I would seduce you, and we would give her the perfect little grandbabies she has been dreaming about since we were kids."

"What?" I sputtered, sitting up higher before I inhaled water.

"That came out wrong," Lily laughed, letting her face fall into her cupped palms. "What I meant was that my mom always thought we would end up together or something. Maybe she saw this as our chance." Lily peeked at me and shrugged.

"Well...I never knew that."

"I never told you."

With nothing to say, I took a drink of my Coke. Good to know I had her mom on my side. Then again, maybe Lily was wrong and Ms. Holladay gave up on me around the same time Lily did.

"The days seem to by flying by much faster here than back home." Lily dragged a hand through the bubbles. "What do you want to do tomorrow? Any wild plans you want to get out before your dad comes up?"

I could only think of one, that included Lily and me naked in my bed, but that was quickly shoved aside when the friend part of me—the guy who had known her since we were in diapers—took over.

"If you're saying you want to throw some crazy party, get it out now."

Lily snorted. "I couldn't even stand Hunter's party. Besides, why would I want a bunch of people defiling this amazing hot tub. I'd never be able to get in it again." She kicked back her head, letting her body float up to the surface.

Her legs skimmed mine on the way up, making my heart flutter at the soft touch. If I didn't know any better, if I wasn't convinced she was only being nice for sake of our truce, I could have sworn she was flirting with me.

My gaze drifted up from her bright-blue toenails to her slightly parted thighs. I slammed my eyes shut and forced my thoughts onto something else, something boring before I had a problem I was certain she would notice. And I didn't want to spend all night in the hot tub.

"I say we spend tomorrow having a movie day. Fat pants and all." Lily popped up out of the water, bringing her face close to mine and settling her hands on the top my thighs. Her hair clung to her shoulders in clumps, sending beads of water down her collarbone to her fantastic...

"What do you say, Hayes?"

I blinked a few times, trying to clear my thoughts, but I couldn't stop my gaze from drifting to her lips. She had a scar on her chin right below her bottom lip from a spill she took after I dared her to race me down an impossibly steep hill a couple of miles from the lake. She didn't talk to me for almost a week. We were eleven, and it was the longest we ever went not speaking...until we were thirteen.

Until the summer we stopped being friends.

I swallowed hard, my throat cramping from how tight it had gotten. Lily looked at me expectantly. Her body caging mine in. Somehow, I figured the look wasn't about the movie proposal.

Her hand drifted up my arm. The featherlight touch left goose bumps in its wake. "Is that a yes or no?" Her tongue trailed across her lip, leaving it glistening in the moonlight.

All I wanted to do was take that full, bottom lip between my teeth and prove once and for all she wasn't capable of hating me. Not when I could make her feel so good.

But my body had other plans. Or I should say my brain.

I jumped out of the water like I had been electrocuted. I might as well have been with how fast my heart was racing. It never even got to that speed during one of my dad's murder practices.

Lily's face fell as I reached for my shirt. "Sorry, I'm not feeling so good. Let's, uh, let's play tomorrow by ear, okay? I think I ate too much junk food or something. I'm not used to it."

I left her there in the hot tub, staring at me like I had run over her dog.

Any chance I had with her was eradicated the second I turned down her very obvious offer.

I had never felt like more of an idiot. I left the girl I had dreamed about for years hanging because for some reason I had a hunch she was messing with me. Getting me back for all the years I had screwed with her. It would be the perfect revenge if she knew how deep my feeling went past friendship.

And somehow, I had an inkling she knew after our moment on the couch.

ELEVEN
Lily

I COULDN'T BEAR to get out of the bed next morning. So, I didn't. I lay there until midafternoon, replaying the night over and over in my head.

Each time it got more cringeworthy.

I had thrown myself at Parker and he turned me down so fast my head spun. Literally running out of the hot tub as if he might catch something.

And the worst part, I had no idea why I did it. Nostalgia. That was the only explanation. Playing our old favorite game. Talking about our childhood. Being on the water. All those old feelings rushed to the surface and, once again, he slapped me in the face with them.

There was no way he wouldn't use it against me the next chance he got.

I sent Madison my seventh SOS-text of the day. Being the brat she was, it changed to *read*, but I never got a response. No three dots to let me know she at least acknowledged my mortification. No best-friend words of advice. Knowing her, she wanted me alone on Parker Island hoping that our hate would turn into lust. If she had been there to witness my epic fail, she would already have rescued me.

The door across the hall opened, and for three agonizing seconds I waited, expecting a knock on my door.

Parker wouldn't be able to last long without throwing what he considered desperation in my face. But it never came. Instead, I heard the front door slam closed and a few minutes later the sound of a car starting up.

My heart pole-vaulted into my throat at the thought of him ditching me. Totally a Parker move.

I rolled off the bed and stumbled across the floor, flinging the door open with shaky hands.

Did I want him to go?

Of course, I did. Why wouldn't I? Parker had been a thorn in my side since eighth grade, and no amount of nostalgia or rippling muscles would change that.

A peek across the hall told me what I needed to know. A pair of jeans lay in a crumpled mess on his equally messed-up sheets. His bag also sat in the corner, tucked under his nightstand.

Okay, so he didn't ditch me. Maybe he needed the same space I did. After all, whatever went down in the hot tub was confusing as hell to me. He must have been thinking the same thing.

With a heavy sigh, I pressed a palm against my forehead. This could work. I could get through the week and the rest of the summer without Parker knowing about my severe lapse in judgment. All I had to do was find an attractive guy and let Parker see it. No harm, no embarrassing retelling when school started.

Since Parker left, it gave me the perfect opportunity to slip out and go find Mr. Hottie. Lakefront was the ideal place. I could only hope that Milo wasn't there. Parker's big, ol'e lie could spread faster than mono at one of Hunter's parties if he caught me out there flirting sans Parker.

Stupid Parker.

I yanked on my suit, deciding at the last minute to leave

behind my cover-up. Sure, it had become a security blanket, and showing so much skin wasn't a habit of mine. But I couldn't look like a frumpy mess if I wanted to draw attention. Not with the likes of Tracy McHugh and her new *life preservers* hanging around. The girl was drop-dead gorgeous before getting a hand with her shortcomings.

The trek to the shore was peaceful, beautiful even. I hadn't noticed before, but there had been several new houses built in the time I was away. Even with the additions, it didn't detract from the natural beauty of the lake. Most of the houses were made to resemble log cabins. Gigantic log cabins, but they still held the same charm. They ended up blending in with the trees instead of sticking out like a sore thumb. The amount of money these people had to have spent was mind-boggling. Parker's house had been in the family forever, purchased and built before his dad was born. That's why all of Mr. Hayes renovations made sense.

His house must have been the old-timer on the block compared to the new and updated versions. But still, it made me sad. Why would his dad want to erase all the good memories just to fit in better?

Lakefront was bursting with bodies, I noticed as I lumbered down the embankment, searching for a place to settle in and scope out a possible flirt buddy.

I spotted Tracy by the waterfront, spraying her already-tanned body with sunblock. Not as if she was hard to miss with her neon-yellow bikini and the gaggle of guys practically drooling at her feet. Okay, jealousy talking, but didn't they care that her hair was bleached that color and half-fake just like her chest? I saw her at the salon once getting enough hair sewn into her head to make a horse envious.

Seriously, were guys only interested in the Instagram-perfect girls? Because if that was the case, I was screwed. I couldn't remember the last time anything but scissors touched my hair. Sure, it got its own platinum highlights from the sun, but it was nowhere near as beautiful as the colors women could get from hairstylists. My mom tried to take me once before freshman homecoming. I took one look at the prices and laughed my ass right out of the shop.

Did she realize how many books I could buy with that money? And let's not forget about shoes. I distinctly remember thinking she was out of her mind, which was funny because she looked at me the same exact way on the drive home and muttered her favorite line about them thinking I was a boy on the sonogram, and how I should have been born that way.

My poor mom, all she wanted was a girly-girl like her. Instead, she got me. But my dad seemed to be happy with that, at first, seeing as I would rather watch football with him than play with dolls.

In the end, even that wasn't enough to keep him around.

I scowled at Tracy and hooked a left, taking me farther away from her and up toward the only other open spot in the area.

A girl in a green one-piece smiled as I unfurled my towel. She didn't look familiar, which meant she didn't go to my school. Not unheard of, people traveled from all over to spend time on the lake.

"Jayla." The girl gave me a small salute as she propped herself up on her elbows. "You look about as uncomfortable as I feel."

"Lily." I pointed at my chest as I dropped down on my towel. "That obvious? Beaches aren't really my thing."

"Me either, but my dad wanted to do something different this year. Most of the time I convince him to take me to Disneyland or camping, but no, he wanted to rent a boat and teach me to water-ski like he did as a kid."

"How's that going?"

"Do you see him or a boat around?" Jayla sat up and slid her sunglasses up to rest on her head. "I nearly broke my neck, I shit you not. Nope. I'm good. I prefer to watch the water at a safe distance."

Jayla was quickly becoming my new best friend since mine went MIA.

"Where do you go to school?" I reached into my bag and pulled out a water bottle. It was way too hot out.

"I go to Eatonville. It's in the middle of nowhere. So being around a bunch of kids I don't know is a little unnerving. My brother was around here, but he ditched me to go do something with a group of guys he met. No doubt includes burping and setting something on fire."

"Yeah, my friend ditched me, too." Wait, did I just call Parker my friend? I shook my head and focused on the water bottle, rolling it between my palms.

"Speak of the devil." Jayla jumped up and shouted at a group of guys making their way over. "Hey, asswipe! You left your stuff here, which means that I had to stick around waiting for you to get back. I didn't know looking at a boat took two hours."

"Chill out, Jay." A tall, muscular guy who looked around my age made his way through the crowd. "I'm back now, so you can go home and continue binge-watching whatever sappy show had you hugging your blanky earlier."

"You're a dick." Jayla bent down to collect her things and sent me a tight smile. "It was nice meeting you."

"Who's this?" Her brother threw an arm around her shoulders as she stood up. Now that he was closer, it was obvious they were twins down to the towering height, which I hadn't noticed when Jayla was sitting.

"This is no one. Go back to your burping contest."

"I'm Lily," I said it without thinking and tried not to acknowledge the dirty look Jayla sent my way.

After brushing one of his dreads off his forehead he extended a hand down to me. "Jayden."

My eyebrows shot in the air. Jayla and Jayden?

"I know," he answered my unspoken thought. "Our parents suck. It wasn't bad enough that I had to share a womb with her." Jayla stuck her tongue out at him. "But then they gave us such similar names, it confused our teachers for most our lives."

"Why don't you go by nicknames then?" I asked, standing to join them because looking up was starting to give me a headache with the sun in my eyes. I was in such a rush, I had left my sunglasses behind on the kitchen counter.

"Because it annoys her to no end that I won't go by something else, and since she was born first, she says she has rights to the name."

"And I do." Jayla slung her tote onto her shoulder. "You staying out here then?" she asked her brother. He gave her a nod and smiled in my direction. "Whatever, be home by dinner because I'm not going out looking for you again."

With that, she stomped off, leaving Jayden there smiling at me.

"So." He plopped down on my towel. "What are you doing out here alone?"

I shrugged and joined him. "My mom forced me to come up here with the family that lives next door. He ditched me so I figured I might as well take advantage of the sun and water."

"Well, he's an idiot then."

"What do you mean? I mean totally, but why do you say that?"

Jayden smiled. "Why would he leave such a beautiful girl out here alone? He's either blind, an idiot, or goes for a different persuasion. So, I went with idiot."

"Wow," I giggled, bending forward to grab my knees. "Does that usually work?"

"Usually." Jayden joined in on the laughter, leaning forward so that his face was close to mine. "But seriously, you guys aren't like...you know?"

"No. God, no." I waved my hands frantically in the air. "We grew up together. Honestly, I think my mom just wanted me out of the house. I haven't even talked to the guy in four years."

"Well, that's good news for me." Jayden pushed my wayward bangs out of my face. "Have any plans for the afternoon?"

I felt my cheeks warm and not from the sun. Jayden was full-on flirting with me in plain sight on a beach swarming with hot girls. At my school, I would have had to strip naked and run down the halls just to compete. And even then, most of the guys would have given me one look, then continued on their merry way.

"Well...I was thinking about playing a game of pool, but then I was ditched. Can't play pool alone." I shot him what I hoped was a flirty look. Judging by the smile on his face, I was doing better than expected.

"I love pool! We used to have a mini one in the garage until my dad decided he wanted to restore an old Challenger. I haven't played in years because the only other place in town that has any is in a bar and they won't let me in."

"Well, it is kind of hot. Want to come play?" Wait... did that come out totally wrong?

Jayden grinned and reached for my hand, standing up in the same movement. "Hell, yeah."

I gathered up my stuff with a growing lump forming in my stomach. Okay, yes, I had planned on finding a guy to prove to Parker I wasn't the least bit interested in him. And Jayden wasn't hard on the eyes, but the way he smiled down at me and gripped my hand. It was almost enough to change my mind. I didn't want to hurt him in the process. Then again, it was a summer fling. No one got attached at the lake. That's why there were just as many hookups as there were breakups.

My thoughts ran a mile a minute, trying to come up with a list of pros and cons on the fly. That was, until I saw the boy standing next to Tracy fiddling with the string on her bikini top. Freaking Parker. Seeing him with her solidi-fied my plan. If I didn't make it clear that he meant nothing to me, and made sure my own brain knew that, he would make my life a living hell. Ten times worse than he had before.

I entwined my fingers with Jayden's and tugged him toward the house. A little pool and flirting never hurt anyone.

As I was making my way up the embankment, I caught Parker's gaze. Even from where I stood, I could have sworn I saw a frown on his face. It only lasted a minute before Tracy threw her head back and laughed, drawing his attention to her.

But the smile on his face was forced in a way I hadn't seen since the day he stood next to his dad and greeted his extended family in that sad, black suit.

Jayden's ball banked off the side and hit mine, sending it straight into the corner pocket. I laughed and poked him with the clean end of the pool stick. He may have had a pool table at his house, but he wasn't very good at it.

"Are you on my team or something? Because you keep sinking my balls." I gave him a little wink as I bent over to line up my shot. He had been doing such a bad job that after a measly five minutes, I only had two balls left on the table.

"It's at an angle, I'm telling you!" He took a drink of his Coke, shaking his head as I laughed and made my shot.

"It's okay to admit you're terrible at something. You can't be great at everything, you know."

Jayden growled playfully and crunched the empty can on the counter. "The sun was in my eyes."

"Uh-huh." I attempted to sink red seven into the far pocket, but I missed by a mile, causing Jayden to whoop and jump off the barstool.

"Big talk for someone who can't make a wide-open shot."

"Which are you again? Because I thought you called stripes off the break but the number of solids you've sank says otherwise."

"I'm sticking with the sun was in my eyes." Jayden managed to sink one of his balls and sauntered around the table toward me. He leaned in, his breath blowing my hair out of my face. "Or maybe it's just the view."

I scrunched my eyes shut and felt my face warm. Again. It was at least the tenth flirty comment he had thrown my way and I had to admit, the boy was smooth. Maybe a little *too* smooth. I would never be able to keep up with him. Parker would see right through it.

"Why don't we call a tie on this game? I saw a nice hot tub out on the deck." Jayden leaned on his pool stick and arched an eyebrow.

Images of my rejection in the hot tub the night before surfaced, forcing a lump to form in my throat. "I'm not letting you off that easy."

Jayden groaned and nudged me out of the way. "Fine. But after I win, we take a dip."

"And when you lose, what then?"

"You're feisty as all hell." Jayden tugged on the sundress I had thrown on over my bathing suit when we got back to the house. "I like it."

His gaze locked on to mine, and I felt my breath stutter as he leaned down toward me. I wasn't planning on kissing him. Not with my original plan. But I couldn't deny how attractive I found him. The boy could have been a model and he knew it, but instead of being a complete ass like most of the boys at my school, he had a genuine demeanor about him. His smile didn't seem forced and his playful banter came naturally. So, yeah, I had to admit I was a little smitten, especially since all that flirting power was directed at me.

I wet my lips and he tracked the motion with his eyes, letting out a little groan as he tipped his head to the side. My hands gripped the pool stick as I closed my eyes and waited for the pressure of his lips on mine.

Instead, a throat cleared from somewhere in the room, and in a rush of wind I felt Jayden move to the side.

My eyes focused on the figure in the doorway. The angry figure. Yikes, I couldn't recall ever seeing that expression on Parker's face. His glare was directed at Jayden, hands clenched into fists for a few seconds past awkward before he concentrated his anger on me.

"Who's this?" He tipped his chin in Jayden's direction, keeping his eyes on me.

"This is Jayden. We met at the lake." I set my pool stick on the table and did my best not to wither under his stare. Seriously, if looks could kill, I would have fallen victim in a heartbeat.

"You must be the guy Lily is staying with." Jayden took a step forward, extending his hand.

"I must be that *guy*." Parker's gaze traveled to him for a split second before sliding back to me. He ignored the offer of a handshake and Jayden let his hand fall back to his side. "And Lily should know that we can't have visitors at the house when my dad is out."

"Oh shit, man, I'm sorry. We just wanted to get in a game of pool."

I flinched under Parker's unyielding glare. Part of me wanted to get Jayden out of the house fast so I could defuse the situation. The other part of me wanted him to stay because I was fairly certain Parker wouldn't go off on me with someone there. It still didn't explain why Parker was so pissed though. Unless his dad had given him that rule, and I went ahead and broke it.

"Well game is over, unfortunately." Parker crossed his arms and leaned against the doorframe.

"Sure, man, no problem." Jayden turned, giving me a weak smile. "Maybe I can get your number? I'm out here for a few more days. We're going out on the boat tomorrow if you want to join."

"We have a boat, but thanks, Jayden," Parker answered for me.

I shot him my own dirty look as I held out my hand. "Sure, give me your phone and I'll put my number in."

Jayden fumbled for it, glancing between us uncomfortably as I typed in my number.

"So...I'll call you?" His words came out as a question as he gathered up his stuff.

Something told me that he wouldn't be calling me. Especially after he bolted from the room, taking the stairs two at a time.

I stood at the top of the staircase a few seconds after the front door slammed shut. I could feel Parker's glare attempting to burn a hole through my back, but I suddenly didn't have the energy to face the inevitable blowup.

Plan successful, I guess? Only instead of seeming relieved that he didn't have to turn me down to my face, Parker seemed pissed.

TWELVE

Parker

I STILL COULDN'T BELIEVE what I walked in on. Sure, I'd seen them leave together, but I never figured I would come home to them all cozy and on the verge of a kiss. Especially not after the weird moment in the hot tub. Unless I had read *way* too much into it.

Lily avoided my eyes as she came back into the room and began cleaning up. She tossed the two empty pop cans into the trash, then hung up the pool sticks on the far wall. As of late, I couldn't read her. One minute she was hot, the next she was cold and distant. I would blink and she would flirt, and then the next moment she showed up at my house with another guy. A guy she didn't know who could have done anything he wanted to her with no one around to stop it.

In an instant, my blood boiled. An image of him on top of her popped into my head and refused to leave, making me angry and confused at the same time. Maybe that's what she wanted. A guy to screw during summer vacation. After all, I hadn't seen her with a boyfriend since sophomore year. Maybe her new thing was a quick hookup. No wonder she gave in and came to the lake.

Lily finally turned to me after she had racked the balls.

Her teeth nibbled on her lower lip as she fidgeted from one foot to the other.

"Would you just say something? Anything?" she blurted out, then took a deep breath. "You're freaking me out just standing over there staring at me."

"What were you thinking?" My words came out harsher than I expected, and it caught her off guard.

"W-what are you talking about?"

"Lake guy. Do you know anything about him? Or are you in the habit of inviting strangers back to your place? That your new thing? Bang it out and move on with your life?"

Lily looked like she had been slapped, her face turning pink all the way up to her ears. "You're one to talk. That's all you ever do. I can guarantee I know more about Jayden than you did about little Miss 'Oh God! Oh God!' Classy."

She was referring, of course, to Alexis Woodall who threw herself at me during a bonfire party last spring. We may or may not have gotten better acquainted in the bed of Hunter's truck. But that was consensual, and I had known her, or I should say *of* her all year.

When I didn't say anything right away, Lily smirked. "That's what I thought. So don't go throwing stones when you live in a glass house, Parker. You're bound to get cut."

She made a move to step around me, but I grabbed her arm, halting her. "He could have hurt you."

"Since when do you care?" She ripped her arm free and took a step back. Her face wavered between hurt and angry.

"I've *always* cared." Saying those words out loud physically hurt. It was a secret I wanted to take with me to the grave. I never planned on telling her how long I held a flame for her. Flirting aside, I had always cared about her and, unbeknownst to her, I had kept tabs on her to make sure she was okay, and that whatever boyfriend she had was taking care of her. Of course, there hadn't been anything to keep track of for the past couple of years. But that didn't stop me from checking in.

"Please." Lily crossed her arms over her chest and leaned away from me. "You dropped me the second you found a cooler group and never looked back. I *needed* you that summer, and I get that you were going through things too, but instead of leaning on me, you ran away. You broke my—" Lily clamped her mouth shut, biting her lips together and cutting off her words.

Words I was pretty sure included her heart.

"I never meant to hurt you. I just—"

"Well, you did. So, you don't get to drop back into my life four years later and get all protective and jealous."

"Jealous?" My anger flared again at the fact that she picked up on my emotions so easily. So easily, in fact, I was scared she would figure out the biggie I kept hidden and throw it in my face. "I wasn't jealous so you can check your ego. I was worried that some lake bum was gonna trash my place or steal some shit after doing the one thing I'm sure he had planned for you."

"You're an ass."

"And you're an oblivious airhead. Guys don't just come back to someone's place to play pool."

"Guys like you don't, Parker. But believe it or not, not everyone is a pig."

We both glared at each other, breathing heavily from rising anger. I wanted to leave her standing in her own irritation just as much as I wanted to kiss her. Years of hiding my emotions left me unstable when I had to face them.

"I want you to take me home tomorrow," she growled.

"No."

Lily's eyes widened and her mouth dropped open. She was used to getting her way, and in the past week, I had shown her that her way or the highway wasn't how life worked.

"No?" She took a step toward me, her anger palpable. "You dragged me up here under false pretenses." She caught the brief guilty look that flashed across my face, judging by the shift in her posture. "Yeah, don't think for one second I believed your dad got called in last-minute. You knew damn well he did, but you brought me up here anyway just to torture me."

"That's not why!" I shouldn't have said that, and the moment I did, I wished I could take it back. Lily could smell blood like a shark, and she zeroed in on it.

"Then why did you bring me up here? And don't tell me it's because you enjoy my company so much because we both know that's a lie."

I couldn't flat-out tell her that's exactly why, so I went with a more believable lie. "Because I was keeping my end of the dare."

"Well the dare is over, you said it yourself. So, you are taking me home tomorrow and we can forget about this whole thing and go back to ignoring each other."

"No." My voice broke in a way that sounded like a toddler mid-tantrum. I hated that she was getting to me, riling me up in a way only she could. "We also had a truce, but I don't see you keeping up your side."

"Truce is over. It was over the second you busted in on my date after fawning all over Tracy out on the water. Hypocritical much?"

"Now who's jealous?" I took a step toward her, watching carefully as the fire in her eyes burned brighter.

She looked like she was on the verge of slapping me, but I didn't care.

"Jealousy would entail me having feelings toward you, which I don't."

"It didn't seem that way yesterday."

There it was, the slight twitch around her right eye that always gave away one of her lies. It was a good thing her parents never figured it out, because we would have been busted on plenty of occasions when doing something we weren't supposed to do. But I had picked up on it when we were nine.

"Screw you, Parker." She shoved her hands into my chest, knocking me backward out of surprise.

I grabbed her wrists as she went to hit me again, pulling her against me so she couldn't lunge at me like she had in the living room. The next thing I knew my lips were crashing into hers. Or maybe it was hers crashing into mine. Rough and raw and still everything I had ever hoped for.

Lily's hands reached for my chest again. For a second I thought she was about to push me away, but instead her fingers knotted in my shirt, pulling me toward her. An involuntary groan escaped me as I slipped my tongue past her lips, testing the waters to see how she would react. She responded with a moan of her own, not only allowing me to deepen the kiss, but brushing her tongue against mine in an expert motion that left me wondering where the hell she learned it.

"Parker..." Lily gasped, as I broke away to trail kisses down her neck. The moment was everything I had ever dreamed about, and I wasn't about to let an opportunity slip by. If she hated me after, I would at least have as many sensations as I could hold on to.

Lily gripped my shoulders as I hoisted her legs up and

wrapped them around my waist. Her back pressed into the green felt as I set her down on the pool table. Her legs remained hooked around me, anchoring my hips to hers and it took every bit of strength I possessed not to lose my ever-loving mind when they bucked into me.

Her hands dropped to my back, pulling me closer, fusing our chests as she tortured me with the slow twist of her tongue. If I had known it would be that good, I would have set aside my pride sooner. Though *good* was a serious understatement.

One of my hands drifted to her thigh, gliding up her smooth skin toward her hip before bringing it back to her knee. As much as I wanted to take the act further, I wouldn't, not with her feelings of hate suspended in the air. I wouldn't want to be a regret she had. That would kill me.

In the distance, I heard what sounded like a door slamming. Footsteps. A voice. Definitely a voice.

"Parker? Lily?"

We flew apart with impressive speed. Lily pulled down her dress as I wiped a quick hand across my lips and knocked the balls out of the rack. Seconds before my dad entered the room, I grabbed a ball and leaned over, pretending that I was setting up for a game of pool.

My dad stepped through the door and stopped. "There you guys are. I've been calling your names."

"Dad." I dropped the eight ball and forced a smile. "You're here early."

I shot Lily a wary glance, praying she wouldn't totally give us away. The deep flush in her cheeks and the way she kept fidgeting told me we would be dead if my dad took a closer look.

"Yeah, we wrapped up early, and I figured I might as well head up. This way we have all Saturday on the water.

Plus, I have a surprise." He made his way to the bar, not giving us a second glance.

And why would he? As far as he was concerned, we were friends who drifted apart. Not hormonal teenagers who had been dangerously close to breaking every rule he had laid out for me. A big one being, don't mess around in his house.

Thus, the bed of the pickup truck.

"I felt bad that I left you guys hanging. It couldn't have been too much fun holed up here alone."

"Dad, we aren't kids anymore. We have a car, and you sent plenty of money. We had fun. Don't feel bad."

Lily's face darkened, and she hid it with a brush of her hair.

"I get it. I still felt bad for bailing, so I talked to Hunter and told him to invite some of your friends for a party tomorrow night. Might as well break the place in, right?"

"A party? Here? Really?" My dad had never been big on parties. He said they were a waste of time.

"Why not? After this week, you'll be so deep into swimming practice you won't have time."

There it was.

Little did my dad know I had no plans to follow through with his body-breaking schedule.

"I talked to your mom, Lily. She called Madison and invited her, but if you have anyone else in mind, feel free. There's plenty of room.

"Okay. Yeah. Sure." Lily kept her gaze fused to the ground and my dad shot her a curious look before pouring a glass of scotch.

"You guys breaking in the pool table?"

I nearly choked on a laugh. Yeah, we were just not in the way he meant. Lily bit down on her lip and glanced in my direction. Her face was beet red. I had to get her out of there before she gave us away. But before I could speak, she made a swift exit.

"I'm going to go call Madison, see when she'll be up here," she called over her shoulder.

Of course she ditched me. I groaned internally and leaned up against the bar.

"A party, huh? Since when are you big on parties?"

"I just thinking that you missed your birthday this year due to district tournaments, and since school and swimming will take up most of your senior year, I figured why not have a bash while we're up here. This house could use some fun —it's been years."

Yeah, I had missed my birthday but not because of the tournament. My birthday fell on a Sunday, but my dad was so hell-bent on keeping my diet and practice on schedule he wouldn't even let me have a small kick-back. I was practically a prisoner, and I couldn't wait to graduate and get the hell out.

"That's nice, Dad. I'm sure everyone will love to have a few days on the lake."

My dad nodded and took a sip of his drink. "So, how have the last few days been? Sorry I couldn't get the boat out for you, but at least you had the Jet Skis. Lily doing okay?"

"Everything is fine, Dad. We took the skis out one day and have just kind of been chillin'. The shore has been crowded so we've avoided it."

"You break in the new hot tub?"

"Uh-huh." If I hadn't run away from Lily, I would have broken it in a hell of a lot better. I tossed the triangle in the middle of the table and scooped up the balls, praying that this conversation would come to an end.

"Lily has grown up to be quite a young lady."

"Young lady?" I winced. "Please. Don't."

"I talked to Ms. Holladay before I left. Did you know that not only is she on the honor roll, but she regularly volunteers at the animal shelter and the children's ward in the hospital? She brings in books and reads to them. I tell ya, that girl has always been too sweet for her own good. The kind of girl you should keep an eye out for in college."

Yup, the conversation definitely needed to end. Not only did I know all those things about her, because I had, in fact, kept tabs on my ex-friend's life, but how could I explain that I wouldn't be looking for a girl *like* Lily when all I wanted was her. No replacements. No carbon copies. I wanted Lily and, judging from her reaction, she wanted me too. It might have been clouded in hate, but I could work with that.

So, I said what I always said when my dad brought up girls. "I'm not getting married, Dad. Not for a long time."

"Of course." He waved away my statement and filled up his glass again. "Just want you to keep an eye out. Your mother isn't here to give her blessings so I get to dole out all the wisdom she would have. And your mother adored Lily."

Ice filled my veins. I hated when he talked about her like that. Four years had passed, but I didn't need him reminding me that she wouldn't be around to gush about my girlfriends. Thus, the reason I had stuck to a strictly non-serious relationship MO.

"What time did Hunter say he would be up?"

"Hmm? Oh." My dad blinked out of a daze and focused on me. "He said late afternoon. If there are any other kids you know up here, invite them. I'll go early and get stuff for the grill."

"Sounds good." I gave him a fake smile and made my way to the door. "See you tomorrow."

A party with my dad sounded like hell on earth. A party with my dad, Hunter, and a bunch of classmates that would no doubt find a way to reverse all the progress I had made with Lily... That sounded like the freaking apocalypse, relationship edition.

THIRTEEN

Lily

"You're such a bitch. You realize that?" I caught the bag of marshmallows Madison tossed my way and stepped back as she climbed out of her beat-up Civic.

"Oh, you love me."

"You left me stranded here with no lifeline. A return text would have been nice. That's what best friends are supposed to do."

Madison grinned as she popped her trunk. "And a best friend is also supposed to make you realize when you're being an idiot. Which you are. Judging from those texts, I know for a fact that you have a thing for Mr. Next-Door Hottie."

"You mean the text that begged you to come get me because he's an asshole? Makes sense, Maddy."

"Uh, no." Madison hoisted a bag way too big for one night onto her shoulder. "I'm judging that based on you throwing yourself at him in the hot tub. Super classy by the way."

"Screw you." I shoved her, but she just laughed.

I failed to mention the whole make-out sesh the night before, mostly because I still didn't understand it, and I knew she would glow as if I had told her that unicorns existed. It was bad best-friend protocol that I didn't immediately call her, but I didn't know what to say. One minute we were yelling and accusing each other of being jealous, and the next Parker's lips were everywhere and I was tempted to rip off his shirt and feel his muscles without the pretense of a Jet Ski.

And the worse part was, I didn't mind it. I loved it, actually. I didn't wake up regretting or hating him. I woke up with a knot in my stomach because if his dad hadn't walked in when he did, we would have given the screws on that pool table a test run that I'm sure they didn't account for at the factory.

"Uh...hello?" Madison waved her hand in front of my face. "Did you hear anything I just said?"

Not at all. I cringed. "No. Sorry."

"You feeling okay?" She pressed her hand to my forehead, but I batted it away.

"I'm fine. What did you say?"

"I said that you might want to find Parker and tell him to go with the whole dating thing tonight. I know you said he called it off, but Hunter will be here, and Hunter isn't going to let it go."

"Oh. Right. Yeah, I'll find him before everyone gets here. Thanks for coming early by the way."

"Duh." She started walking toward the house and I fell in line beside her. "It gives me more time to get dolled up. Who knows what kind of eye candy there will be?"

"It's pretty much the same people we've gone to school with since elementary."

"Eww, not them. The guys at the beach. I plan on finding my own hottie, since I'm assuming you'll be ditching me for a piece of Parker pie."

I stumbled and struggled against a laugh. Egging her on

was always a bad idea. "Dear God, Madison, where do you come up with this stuff?"

She shrugged and sent me a mischievous smile as we stepped into the house. "Where am I unloading at?"

"You can bunk with me." I pointed to the bedroom and took the grocery bag she had. "I'll put this stuff in the kitchen.

Madison winked before heading off in the direction I pointed her. I hung back and surveyed the area. One additional thing I forgot to mention to her...I had been avoiding Parker since the kiss, which had become increasingly difficult when his dad seemed to be all over us, trying to get us to do group outings. I had already spent all morning alone on the shore with earbuds in, praying for no run-ins with Jayden or Milo.

We still needed to talk about the whole thing, but I preferred to do it without his dad hanging around, not to mention a houseful of schoolmates.

Madison was right, though. I should mention the dating dare sooner rather than later. We would have to dust it off for the party to be safe. I only hoped that didn't lead to a talk about the kiss because I was nowhere near ready to talk about it.

It was great and hot and made my knees weak. But he was still Parker, my sworn enemy. A boy who hated me nearly as much as I hated him. Hated being past tense. Over the past few days those feelings of revulsion had lessened. They were not completely gone, but enough that I could think of him in another way.

I tossed the grocery bag on the counter, so absorbed in my thoughts I didn't hear the footsteps behind me. Bad trait of mine.

"Hey."

I jumped and spun around, almost dropping the container of potato salad. "Parker. Hey." My heart did a cartwheel forcing me to concentrate on keeping my thoughts off my face. I had a bad habit of being transparent when something was on my mind. Especially with Parker.

"I didn't mean to scare you. Madison said you needed help putting away groceries..." His gaze landed on the one reusable bag on the counter and his eyebrows shot up.

Freaking Madison. Of course she said that.

"Oh, no. I got it."

Parker nodded, his eyes lingering on my face for a couple of extra seconds before turning to leave.

"Wait." He halted and turned to face me. It might have been my own apprehension, but I could have sworn he looked nervous, which made me more nervous. "Um... Madison—she brought up a good point about Hunter being here."

"What about Hunter?" Something passed through Parker's eyes with such speed, there and gone in an instant, that I was left thrown.

"Well...the whole dare thing. I know you said to drop it, but maybe it would be a good idea to pretend it was still going? I don't want to make a scene."

Parker crossed his arms over his chest, and damn it if the fabric didn't groan from how tight it pulled over his muscles. "You want to pretend to date me again?"

"Just for tonight. You know...keep the peace."

"Okay." He could not have sounded more disinterested. "Is that all you wanted to talk about?"

My traitorous eyes dipped to his lips. Talking was no longer what I had in mind. What I wanted was to throw him on the counter and give the pool table a run for its money. But that would have to wait until we had talked about what the kiss even meant. Judging from his face—absolutely nothing.

"Yeah."

"Sure, Holladay. I'll be your stand-in boyfriend for the night. Just let me know what you need."

"Whatever. Sure. Just be nice and agree if people ask about the dare."

"Okay.

"Okay. Cool." I rolled the container of potato salad in my hands, savoring the cold on my sweaty hands.

"Is that it?"

"Uh-huh."

Parker nodded his head and left me standing there wallowing in my own mortification. I just asked the guy who clearly hadn't given our kiss a second thought if he would pretend to be my boyfriend for the night. Perfect. Awesome. Not desperate at all.

On second thought, maybe I wouldn't bring up the kiss. If he cared to talk about it, he could bring up. I would just work on forgetting it. Although even as those words formed in my head, so did the memory of his lips on mine and how he stole my breath with a simple touch.

Stupid Parker.

◠───◦

"Come on, Lily. I want to go out on the boat with the boys."

"Then go." I took in her upside-down form as I let my hands fall off the bed and brush the carpet.

I had pretty much hidden in my bedroom most of the afternoon so I could avoid Parker. It worked to my advantage as Madison unpacked and modeled the outfits she had brought for the party, insisting I pick the best one. But once she got word that Parker's dad was taking him and Hunter out on the boat, she got antsy.

There were a few hours until everyone else arrived. Apparently, Hunter invited a good percentage of our class and several girls he met on the shore. I should have been mad, but it would just mean more bodies to separate Parker and me. He agreed, but I wasn't sure how well I would do pretending to be his girlfriend. Not after everything. And so, I planned to hide out in my room until the coast was clear.

"I don't want to go without you," Madison pouted.

"I've had enough of the water. You go and it will give me time to get ready for the party.

Total lie. It's not like I brought anything for a party since I hadn't planned on one. And there was no way in hell I was going to wear one of Madison's outfits. I had enough of that after Hunter's.

"Ugh, fine! Just know you suck as a best friend."

"Love you, too." I blew her a kiss as she stormed out. Five minutes on the water with shirtless Hunter and Parker and she would get over it.

Relief turned sour in my stomach as I pictured her flirting with Parker. She said she was over it and that he was all mine, but the girl loved to flirt. Me not being there would give her an opening. She might even do it just to force me to admit I liked him.

The thought hit me like a lightning bolt.

Shit. I liked him. As in *liked* him.

Damn it. Why did he have to go and make me fall for him again?

I growled and flipped off the bed. If we were on the boat, I would still be able to avoid Parker and keep an eye on her. With that in mind, I made my way to the living room where the boys had been camped out all afternoon entertaining Mr. Hayes with stories of junior year. Well, Hunter was telling the stories and Parker was yelling at him to shut up.

No one was there. I peeked out the window in time to see Mr. Hayes's truck turn the corner with the boat attached.

Crap.

The loading dock was too far for me to walk, so I flopped over the back of the sofa and reached for the remote. At least I didn't have to hide out in my room. Mindless TV would have to do, because if I sat in silence my brain would come up with some very colorful scenarios between Madison and Parker. Then I would drive myself insane.

"Hey."

A squeak jumped out of my mouth as I practically rolled off the couch.

"Parker?" My hand settled on my chest like it could slow the rapid beating of my heart. "What are you doing here?"

"I wasn't feeling the boat, so I told my dad I wanted to set up for the party. What are you doing here?"

"Me, too. Well, not the setting up, but just not feeling the water today."

"Because you're avoiding me?"

Try as I might, I couldn't stop the bulging of my eyes. So busted. "What? No. Of course not."

"Sure, okay." Parker sat in the leather recliner facing me. "Are you at least going to tell me why you're avoiding me?"

"I'm not avoiding you, Parker. Not everything is about you." That's right, when caught, deny, deny, deny.

"If you have something to say, now's the perfect time because no one is around to hear it."

Sometimes, I forgot how well he knew me.

"I...um... No, I mean, nothing is bothering me. You know how I feel about parties." Flustered words fell out of my mouth before I could stop them. The fact that I was lying was crystal clear in my stuttering tone.

"So, you're mad I'm throwing one? Because it wasn't my idea, you know, and my dad is hard to say no to."

I brushed off his statement with a wave of my hand. "Of course not. I know how he gets. I just need to mentally prepare for it. I didn't want to be all sunburned and tired."

"And you expect me to buy that?"

"Why not?" I sat up, tucking my feet underneath me. "It's the truth."

Sticking to the lie no matter what. Only thing to do when the alternative is utter embarrassment.

"You avoiding me has nothing to do with last night?"

Oh, so busted. Why did he have to know me so well?

"Why would it? It was just a stupid kiss, Parker." *Liar, liar, pants on fire*. I tried to make my words come out nonchalant, but instead they had a sharp edge to them as if I really couldn't care less. Which was so far from the truth it might as well be in its own galaxy.

"Stupid..." Parker's brow pinched together for a second as he watched me. After a few beats he smiled. "Right. Totally stupid. I'm glad you agree. I was worried there for a second."

"So... We're okay? I mean back to friends?" We weren't even friends to begin with, so I wasn't sure how we could go *back* to that, but it was the first thing I thought of.

"Friends, yeah, of course." Parker stood, wiping his

palms on his gray swim trunks. "I gotta go get everything ready. I'm glad we cleared that up."

"Do you need help?" I moved to get up, but he waved me off.

"Nah. Enjoy the last few peaceful hours until everyone gets here."

Parker jogged up the stairs, leaving me to stare at his tense, retreating back.

That conversation could not have gone worse. I didn't mean anything that I said.

And as I sat there alone, the realization of how much that kiss meant came crashing down. It meant everything. Somehow in a few days, Parker had managed to wiggle back into my life and ignite the long-dead flame I carried for him for so many years. Like turned to love and I once again sat in my own uncertainty.

After the conversation, I was left with a hollow feeling because I had no idea how I would approach it again. Not after we agreed it meant nothing.

Four years later, I was back to wallowing over a guy who would never see me the same way. And after the week was up would probably go back to ignoring me.

FOURTEEN
Lily

"Heads up!"

A pop flew across the deck, landing in the hot tub with a splash.

"You could have handed it to me!" Deacon yelled as he ran his hands through the bubbles searching for the can of Coke.

Hunter shrugged and turned back to his conversation with one of the girls he picked up on the shore. She giggled in an annoyingly over-the-top way and slid her manicured hand down his arm feeding into his already gigantic ego.

Madison caught my eye and rolled hers. "He was insufferable all afternoon. Any time we passed another boat with a group of girls, he made Mr. Hayes pull over so he could talk to them. I'm surprised he didn't invite half the lake here."

"He acts like it's his house." I stretched out on the lounge chair, soaking in the last bit of the sun's rays. My shirt rode up, but I made no move to push it down. Considering most of the girls at the party were wearing skimpy bathing suits, a little belly button from me was hardly an eye-catcher.

"It practically is, right?"

"Hmm?"

"The house. He's been Parker's friend for like four years. They're always together. No wonder Mr. Hayes lets him get away with murder."

"Which is surprising since he thinks friends are a waste of Parker's energy."

Madison took a drink of her pop and rolled her eyes again when the girl's laugh cut through the air. It really was annoying.

"Where is Parker?" Madison asked, adjusting her sunglasses so they sat on top of her head.

I held a palm out. "I haven't seen him since you guys left for the boat."

"Weird that he didn't come. Did he stay behind so he could get a little flirt action in?" Madison wiggled her eyebrows, causing me to laugh so I could cover up my embarrassment when I thought about our conversation.

Flirting with me was the last thing on Parker's mind.

My laughter was cut short when Parker walked in, Tracy McHugh hanging on his arm.

"Eww," Madison mumbled my exact sentiments. "Why is she here?"

Madison and Tracy went way back, starting with the fact that they were best friends in elementary school and ending with Tracy cutting Madison from the cheerleading squad after an act of "indecency", which pretty much meant she caught Madison making out with her ex and became enemy number one.

All that aside, it didn't explain why she was there with Parker. Not when he was supposed to be pretending to go along with the dare.

I tried to catch his eye so I could send him a silent *what the hell*, but he seemed adamant about avoiding eye contact. Tracy on the other hand, didn't.

"Hey, Lily," she called in an overly sweet tone. Seriously, it almost gave me diabetes.

"Hey, Tracy." Madison's nose wrinkled at my greeting, but what was I supposed to do, ignore the girl?

"Isn't this place gorgeous? Parker promised me a thorough tour later."

Yeah, I didn't miss the innuendo in that statement. Neither did the rest of the partygoers judging by the whooping and whistling.

I shook my head. Parker was back to his douchy self. Right in the nick of time to embarrass me in front of Hunter. But to my surprise, Hunter didn't call me out. In fact, he sent a nod in Parker's direction—the universal code for *get it dude*—and went back to talking to his leech...sorry, date.

"That's so gross." Madison gagged and turned away from Tracy.

But I couldn't. It was like a train wreck. No matter how much my chest constricted as she ran a hand up Parker's arm and leaned in to whisper in his ear, I couldn't look away. Not even when he brushed a strand of her overly bleached hair out of her face. And the one thing that kept running through my head was that it should have been me.

If only Parker saw me like that.

If only he loved me back.

"I can't be out here." Madison stood and motioned to the door. "Want to go down to the dock?"

I tore my eyes away from Parker. "Sure." Anything was better than watching Tracy wrap around him like an octopus trapping its meal.

Madison bounded down the stairs and I followed with a lot less enthusiasm. Parker had been insistent all week to butt in when I was talking to a guy, then he kissed me and showed up to the party with another girl. He hadn't changed. Not one bit. He was still the same heartless Parker he had been since eighth grade. Out for his own butt, not caring how he affected anyone else. And he didn't deserve an ounce of my affection.

Of course, thinking that was a hell of a lot easier than making my heart believe it.

Madison made her way to the edge of the dock and plopped down. A few boats littered the water, but other than that the area was peaceful. I sat down next to her and leaned my head on her shoulder.

"Parker is an idiot and I'm sorry I got you messed up with him."

"It's fine." It *really* wasn't. My heart wouldn't be bruised if she hadn't forced him on me.

"I shouldn't have started the whole dare thing. I really thought he had a thing for you, you know? Like, whenever you were around, he couldn't keep his eyes off you."

"Unless something better like Tracy walks in."

"Tracy is *not* better. Okay, sure her boobs are better now but she had to pay for them. Without that, she would just be another girl desperate for attention."

"I kissed him last night." The words flew out of my mouth without prior approval of my brain. Madison stiffened and leaned away to capture my eyes.

"I'm sorry... What?"

"It was stupid and then this afternoon he told me it was exactly that...stupid."

"Wait, hold on." Madison drew her knees to her chest and rested her chin on them. "Explain exactly what happened."

"I met a guy at the lake and invited him here to play pool. Parker walked in, freaked out, and then started accusing me of being jealous because I saw him earlier with Tracy. Then we...kissed. It came out of nowhere."

Madison's eyes looked like they were on the verge of popping out. "And then what?"

"His dad came up early."

"Did he see you guys?"

"Nope. We heard him, thank God. How embarrassing would that have been?"

Madison chewed on her thumbnail like she always did when deep in thought. "I'm confused, though. He breaks up your little flirt-fest, accuses you of being jealous then tells you the kiss meant nothing. That makes no sense."

"Okay, I might have called the kiss stupid first, but he ambushed me and wanted to talk about it. I'm not good at that type of shit."

"Well, how *do* you feel about it?"

I groaned and flopped onto my back. The wood was still warm from the sun even though dusk had set in. "I have feelings for the jerk. I used to have the biggest crush on him before we stopped being friends and this week brought it all crashing back."

"You never told me."

"I didn't tell anyone, so you are sworn to best-friend secrecy." I pointed a finger at her, and she made a cross over her heart. "I planned to tell him the summer my dad left, but his mom had just died, and I figured I had waited years, what would a couple of more months be in a lifetime. But when school started up, I was a nobody to him."

"I don't think that's true. I've seen how he looks at you. There's something there."

"Yeah, annoyance. I was a kiss of convenience. Or boredom. That's it."

"Well, I still think you're wrong. And I can prove it." Madison jumped up and extended her hand to me.

"Oh, no. What plan do you have brewing?"

"Just going to doll you up and flaunt you around. Maybe some hands-on flirting with a guy who isn't Parker. He'll be dropping Tracy like the disease-infested bimbo she is, come the end of this party."

"First," I said, as I got up. "That's a bit harsh. And second, why should I change how I look to make him notice me?"

"We aren't changing you, just giving him a little push. Once he's good and hooked, you can go back to your jeans and hoodies."

"Hey." I pointed to my cutoff shorts. "I'm wearing shorts and a tank top."

"*Jean* shorts." Madison grabbed me by the hand and hauled me toward the house. "One of my outfits is bound to do the trick."

I whined, but she was having none of it. She led me up the stairs and practically threw me into the room once we reached the door.

She wasted no time as she shuffled through her clothes, mumbling to herself about length and colors. For a second, I thought I heard the door to the room down the hall—Parker's childhood room—slam shut, but I was distracted as Madison chucked a bright-blue crop-top at me.

"Nope." I tossed it at her. The thing was purposely shredded, looking like it had been through the garbage disposal.

"No arguing tonight, pretty please?"

I huffed but held out a hand. I could endure a couple of hours of being out of my element if it meant she got off my back. Once she realized I was right and Parker had no feelings at all for me, she would let it go. That was, until she found another guy she wanted to throw me at.

Five minutes later, I fidgeted in front of the mirror. I had talked her out of the skirt that could have doubled as a belt, opting to keep on my own shorts. Paired with the crop top and a ridiculous belly chain, I felt utterly uncomfortable.

"You look smokin' hot." Madison squeezed my shoulders from behind. "He'll never know what hit him."

"So, a bare midriff is going to convince him he wants me and not boobs galore upstairs?"

"Exactly. You just have to show him you're not the girl he grew up with. Maybe he said the kiss was stupid because he kept thinking about you with blisters from the monkey bars."

"Seems like a solid theory, Maddy. Reality says he's just not that into me."

"But he will be," Madison sang as she pulled me out of the room by my arm into the hall.

"And when this fails?"

"*If* this fails, I'll do your calculus homework for a month when school starts."

We made our way to the stairs, and right as my foot touched the landing, Mr. Hayes appeared at the top.

"Hey, Lily. Will you grab a few of the extra folding chairs we have? I stored them in Parker's closet." He mumbled something about needing them five minutes ago as he walked away.

"Sure, Mr. H."

Madison sighed next to me, no doubt because my entrance had been delayed and would be accompanied by a bunch of chairs. I made my way to Parker's room, opening the door with a knock in case anyone was in there. Fair warning for horny teenagers to get off each other in time.

Silence.

Good, I didn't wanna bust out the hose.

Madison flipped on the lights as I slipped open the closet door. I stuck my head inside, but I didn't see any chairs. Just a bunch of boxes.

"Maybe he meant Parker's old room." I turned to Madison who shrugged.

I hated going in there, especially with how far out of the way Parker went to avoid it. We walked the few steps down the hall, and as Madison reached for the handle, a weird, sick feeling took over my stomach. Before I could tell her to wait, she pushed the door open and flipped on the lights.

The sickness turned into full-blown nausea. I took a step backward, running into the wall in the process. Madison's wide eyes met mine, and for a second both of us were rendered speechless.

Tracy let out a little yelp, climbing off Parker's lap, adjusting her bathing suit top in the same movement. Parker jumped up, his mouth falling open then closing several times as he glanced from her to me, eyes wide with embarrassment.

No embarrassment necessary. I'd seen him in worse positions.

"You could knock," Tracy snapped.

Tracy's grating voice unlocked my brain.

So, the kiss had, in fact, meant nothing. I was just a distraction until he got what he really wanted. And that thing was a girl willing to go to his bed. Little did he know I was on the verge of that when he kissed me.

"Sorry," I mumbled and sidestepped to my room. I

wasn't sure why I was apologizing. Especially when I could hear my own heart breaking.

"Lily, wait." Parker reached for my arm, but Madison stepped in between us and shoved him.

"Piss off, Parker. Go back to whatever the hell you were doing. Or should I say *who* you were doing."

"It's not like that," he snapped.

With a rough sweep of my thumb, I knocked away a tear as I reached for my bag. He didn't deserve my tears. I was an idiot to get sucked back in anyway. But I did need to leave. I couldn't be around him anymore—not when I knew how far that little act would have gone behind closed doors if I hadn't interrupted.

"Lily," Parker pleaded from the hall. Tracy appeared next to him, wrapping a hand around his arm.

"Parker," she whined and tugged on him.

He didn't take his eyes off me. His intense, serious eyes. They all but begged me to hear him out. Too bad I was fresh out of caring. With a sigh, I steeled my nerves and marched over to the dresser chanting *Don't cry. Don't cry. Don't cry.* in my head as I packed up my stuff.

"I need to talk to you," he tried again, but Madison was on top of it. She stepped into the room and slammed the door in his face before he could get another word out.

I wasn't sure how we would escape because I was fairly certain he would still be waiting on the other side when I was finished packing, but that's what Madison was there for. Girl was my rock.

"I'll drive you home." Madison reached into the closet, and much like me, tossed her stuff into her bag without folding it. She must have been just as torn up as me, because I had never seen her treat her clothes that way.

"I'll give you gas money."

Madison laughed and then I laughed. I had no idea where that came from. My brain seemed a little fried after the whole scene.

"Hey." She draped an arm over my shoulder, giving me a shake as I zipped up my bag. "Forget about him. He's an asshole."

"Yeah." But he wasn't. This Parker was, but my Parker wasn't. The Parker who I got to spend the past four days with. He was the guy I fell for. I didn't think it was possible for someone to be Dr. Jekyll and Mr. Hyde in real life, but apparently it was.

"Ready?" Madison asked with her hand on the doorknob.

I rolled my shoulders with head held high and nodded.

The first thing I saw was Parker leaning against the wall, eyes downcast. When the light from the bedroom hit him, his head snapped up. The second thing I saw was that Tracy wasn't with him.

Thank God.

"Lily, I need to talk to you. What you saw in there was—"

"You feeling up Malibu Barbie?" Madison finished for him and reached for my hand. "Fulfilling a fantasy of yours to bang a bimbo in your childhood bed?" She yanked me forward, and I followed, trying my best to avert my gaze.

"No, that's not what happened," he yelled from behind me and grabbed my arm.

I could have sworn Madison spit fire as she whirled around to slap his hand away.

"Don't touch her! We're leaving."

"I just need to explain, please."

"Go back to your party, Parker," I called as we bounded down the front steps. Several people had gathered to watch the show. I noticed Tracy standing next to Hunter, her arms crossed over her chest and a pout on her face.

She looked as happy about being interrupted as I felt about walking in on it. With me gone, she could get back to whatever they were doing.

Madison tossed our things into the trunk, shooting Parker a death glare when he came closer.

"Lily, please."

"It's fine," I said as I propped open the passenger side door. "Just another stupid kiss, right?"

His face fell as I climbed inside. It was the last time I allowed myself to look at him. I closed my eyes and immersed myself in "Youngblood" blaring out of Madison's speakers.

Freaking Parker Hayes. It was the last time I let my heart fall for his tricks.

FIFTEEN
Parker

bahaha what!? ↓

I PUNCHED a nearby tree as Madison's taillights turned the corner headed for the highway. It was not how the night was supposed to go down. When I found out Hunter had invited Tracy to the party, I figured a little harmless flirting would make Lily realize our kiss wasn't stupid at all. Tracy was the biggest flirt around. Part of the reason I never hooked up with her. She would already have her sights set on someone new before we even finished.

When my dad asked me to grab folding chairs, Tracy offered to help. I didn't think anything of it until she shut the lights off and closed the door.

Before I could stop her, she pushed me onto the bed and mounted me like I was some kind of prized stallion. I guess in her eyes I was. She'd been through most of the star athletes in our school in the past three years, but our relationship never jumped the line past flirting.

right...

I was in the process of getting Tracy off me when Lily walked in. Tracy had taken the moment before to demonstrate the awesomeness of her new assets. So what Lily saw was a half-naked girl on my lap and not my attempt to remove said girl from her perch.

"What was that?" Hunter asked from my side.

"Nothing, man. A misunderstanding."

"I've never seen Madison so pissed."

Truth. The girl was like a rabid pit bull. Normally, she was more like a fluffy lapdog.

"Everything is messed up."

"I thought you were going to tell Lily how you feel about her tonight?"

Hunter had been privy to my crush on Lily since he was sworn in as best friend material freshman year. It was part of the reason he pushed the whole dare so hard. He wanted to give me a fighting chance. But he also gave me a deadline for telling her, or he would out me.

End of summer.

"I was until Tracy happened."

Hunter glanced over his shoulder where most of the partygoers had gone upstairs. Everyone except Tracy. She stood on the porch, arms still crossed tightly against her chest.

"I told you flirting with her was a bad idea. Girl is like a hyena when she wants something. Nearly broke my dick last year at homecoming."

I groaned, tipping my head back. I royally screwed up. After the years of back and forth I was fairly certain Lily would never forgive me. I wouldn't be surprised if she made her mom move to get away from me.

"So, what now?" I asked Hunter. It wasn't as if he was the king of relationships, but he was my best friend. I needed best-friend advice.

"Now, we go back to the party. You're up here three more days. Let Lily cool down before you try to talk to her. It's not like you don't know where she lives."

"She might set fire to my house or something to get me to move."

Hunter chuckled and slung an arm over my shoulder. "Nah, I would be more worried about Tracy doing that."

Tracy gave me the evil eye as we approached the house. I wouldn't put it past her, either.

Sensing I wasn't in the mood to deal with her, Hunter transferred his arm to her, pulling her in close to whisper something in her ear. Whatever it was made her laugh and drew her manic gaze to him.

Can't beat a loyal best friend.

"Where did Lily go?" my dad asked the second I stepped inside. "I asked her to get the chairs that apparently *you* couldn't handle grabbing. Next thing I knew, I heard she left. I promised her mom I would look after her. She isn't going to like her leaving at night."

"I don't know. I caught her and Madison as they were packing up their stuff, but they wouldn't tell me why." Good thing my dad didn't know me well enough to catch my lie. In fact, most of our conversations included lies. On both ends.

"Maybe boy trouble," Hunter added, as he led Tracy into the kitchen.

I scowled at him. Way too close to the truth for comfort.

"Well, I should call her mom, let her know she's headed back."

"No," I blurted out. Ms. Holladay would figure out something was off the second my dad mentioned boys. "I'll call her."

My dad nodded before someone called for him upstairs. With a pat on the shoulder, he left.

I didn't know what the hell I was going to tell her mom, but I pulled out my phone anyway and dialed. After three rings, she answered. I was really hoping it would go to voice mail.

"Parker?"

"Hey, Ms. Holladay. I just wanted to let you know Lily and Madison are headed home."

I could hear shuffling in the background. Sounded like papers. She was known to work late, especially during the summer when most people bought houses. "What happened? Is she sick or something?"

"No. My dad decided to throw a party. It's just not her scene."

"Oh. It's odd she would drive all the way back home tonight."

Yeah, because I blew her off then threw a girl in her face. But I couldn't tell her mom that. Ms. Holladay had been a surrogate mom for most of my life, even when Lily stopped talking to me. I didn't want to lose that relationship or have the ire of another Holladay woman.

"Yeah, I wanted you to know. Just in case."

"Well, thank you, Parker. I'll give her a call."

My heart stuttered in my chest. I could only hope she didn't tell her mom the truth. Knowing their relationship, she probably would. "Okay... Well, good night."

"Night."

I hung up the phone and tapped it to my forehead. Lily had three days until I came home. Three days to tell her mom everything that happened, or to come up with her own plan to shut me out of her life forever. Judging from the look she gave me as she got into the car that was her exact plan.

Bass from the stereo rattled the walls. People laughed. Balls cracked against each other on the pool table, but I couldn't concentrate. Normally, I loved to lose myself in a party. Shut out the world and all the responsibilities my dad piled on me. After the crap night I had, all I wanted to do was lock myself in my room and go to bed.

Not that sleep would have come. My racing mind made sure of it.

I found myself standing on the threshold of Lily's room. The same room she always used when we were kids. The bed was made, I noticed. She was always that weirdo who made the bed right after getting up. Said it started your day with something productive. As weird as it was, I liked that about her.

With a stuttered breath, I stepped inside and reached for the closet door on the right. I slid it open and took in the many boxes filled with photos that once adorned the walls. My dad stored them during the remodel, and neither one of us had gotten around to putting them back up. For me, it was hard to see both my mom and Lily *everywhere*. Even though I avoided the lake house. For my dad, I think he just wanted to move on. Not forget, which is why he kept the photos, but attempt to continue with his life.

He even dated a few women over the years, but nothing stuck. There was a high chance that had more to do with me. Several of the meetings hadn't gone well. My dad may have been looking for his next wife, but I sure as shit wasn't looking for another mom. The women didn't get that.

I pulled out the top box and sat down with it resting at my feet. For some reason, my hands shook as I flipped open the flaps. The first picture on top was one of Lily and me at Christmas. We sat next to the tree in matching pajamas. Ones with snowmen all over them. My mom loved giving everyone matching pajamas and having a race to see who could put them on fastest. Winner got to be Santa and pass out the presents. Lily won that year. Her Santa hat sat low on her forehead, threatening to fall into her eyes. I had my arm wrapped around her shoulder and Lily was looking up at me with the biggest grin on her face.

We had just turned ten, with her birthday in October and mine in September. Fourth grade and thick as thieves. Most of the time our parents couldn't separate us, and on more than one occasion, we had sleepovers during the week. Since we were right next door, it made it easier, but it didn't stop our parents from making a big deal about it. School nights or something like that.

I let the photo drop to my lap and reached for another. Lily and I held hands at the beach. We couldn't have been older than five. In the distance, my mom did a cartwheel in the surf. My dad must have taken it. Judging by the slightly blurred edges, I was almost certain. He was never very good with the camera.

Our lives were practically intertwined. I spent the next hour going through the photos, remembering the good times before everything broke. A few times someone from the party stopped in to see where I went. Eventually I locked the door.

My dad never came, and I figured on some level he must know what was going on with me. At least I hoped. Our relationship hadn't been the same since he started the renovation without asking me. He wiped away my mom, tossing her in the closet instead of dealing with the pain. He focused all his energy on my swimming, to the point where I couldn't stand it anymore. Or him.

But he was still my dad.

I lay on the floor surrounded by snapshots of my life. One way or another, I would get my life back. Starting with the girl who stole my heart the day she nearly knocked out her teeth on a hill that was way too steep for bikes. All because she couldn't turn down a dare.

SIXTEEN
Lily

THE CHIRPING BIRD outside the window went from annoying to maddening in the span of an hour. All I wanted to do was sleep my vacation away, but the damn thing had other plans. Three days in a row I woke up to the noise. It didn't bother me too much at first. Summer song and all. But it was Tuesday, the day Parker came home from the lake. And I was a bundle of nerves.

I tried to persuade my mom to let me stay over at Madison's, but she gave some lame excuse about me already being gone and wanting me home. I had half a mind to sneak out. But we only had one car, and she took it to work.

Uber was still an option, though...

The bed creaked under me as I rolled over. I expected Parker to have at least sent me a text in the past few days, but nothing. Radio silence. He hadn't even posted any photos on social media, which was strange for him. Not that I was checking or anything.

Hunter did, however, and I was pretty sure I saw enough pictures of Tracy to last me a lifetime. Apparently, her fling with Parker was short-lived. Hours short. By the end of the night, judging by the postings, she ended up in the hot tub with Hunter.

Good thing I was never going back to the lake house,

because I would never be able to look at the hot tub the same let alone get into it. Not without copious amounts of bleach.

My phone chirped from my nightstand. I had half a mind to ignore it, just in case it was Parker. Seeing as he hadn't tried yet, I reached for it, noticing a notification from Madison.

Madison: A guy that I'm pretty sure is a swim-suit model just came into the store

Me: Hot.

Madison: Would it be weird if I told him I could help him try on clothes?

Me: Considering u work in a shoe store...ya

Madison sent me a photo of her making a weird cringe-slash-excited face. In the background was a guy who could pass for a blurry model, bent over, grabbing a pair of shoes.

I rolled my eyes and tossed my phone on the bed. If I responded, it would just encourage her creepy behavior.

At ten in the morning, it was far too early to be up and about, especially during the summer. But considering the bird and my best friend refused to let me sleep away my life like Sleeping Beauty, I got up.

I wasn't going to be happy about it, however.

My mom was long gone—she had an early meeting out of town that would keep her well past dinner. Thus the reason she took the car and didn't carpool like normal. She kept weird hours, but I guess that's what happens when you're a real estate agent. Got to work around client schedules.

I went straight for the kitchen, planning on pouring myself a bowl of sugary cereal, when a noise from outside caught my attention. Before I even reached the window, I knew what I would find.

Parker's Eclipse sat in the driveway. Next to it was Parker, his tight, gray shirt stretched to its max over his back muscles as he unloaded a bunch of stuff from his trunk.

I don't remember bringing that much to the lake.

As if sensing me, his gaze flicked to my window. I ducked out of the way, even though I was pretty sure he couldn't see me with the glare from the sun. But just in case, I pressed into the wall and peeked through the window from the edge of the curtain.

Parker pulled out his phone and typed something in. I heard my phone chime upstairs. I scowled in his direction and let the curtain fall into place. He could go straight to hell. If he thought rolling into town equaled instant forgiveness, he had to be out of his mind.

With a whole day of daytime TV in mind, I threw my hair up in a messy bun and grabbed my bowl of cereal. Madison would be at work until almost five, and by then her parents would want her home for dinner. My mom wouldn't be home at all, not until late, so I figured, why not add another lazy day to the ones I had already compiled.

That was the plan. However, whatever Parker was doing outside was making a hell of a lot of noise. I had to turn up the TV three times before it drowned it out. But by that time, I couldn't get him out of my head.

He didn't deserve another second of my time.

Stupid jerk. I already spent all of Sunday moping and when that didn't help my busted heart, I switched my emotions to anger. An easier emotion to cope with under normal circumstances. With him back, it flared brighter, making me want to go over there and kick him square in the balls.

Alas, doing so would let him know how much he hurt me, how much he burrowed under my skin in the days we spent together. So, I decided instead that I would just revert to old Lily. Main objective: pretending he didn't exist. Him and his stupid, tight shirts, vibrant-hazel eyes, and perfectly floppy hair could go to hell.

I wandered upstairs, needing space from him. Walls and a driveway weren't enough. My phone chirped again, and I picked it up without thinking. Two notifications filled my screen. One from Madison and one from Parker.

My hand shook as my thumb hovered over his name. I *knew* he texted me from outside. So full of himself.

With apprehension and curiosity crowding my belly, I tapped on his message.

Parker: Stop staring at me like a creep & come outside.

Like hell. I quickly deleted all of his messages, then his number, ridding my phone of him so I wouldn't be tempted to respond and egg him on. After a brief moment where I stuck my tongue out in the general direction of his bedroom like a five year old, I clicked on Madison's text.

Madison: Wanna do lunch?

Me: Too broke. No car.

Her reply came a few minutes later as I was making my bed. At this point, it was a surprise she hadn't gotten fired for always being on her phone.

Madison: What if I told u there were a couple of hotties here willing to take us to lunch?

Me: I would still be left with no car.

She sent me the middle finger emoji followed quickly by another message.

No because what is this?

Madison: Movie night at least? The 'rents are driving me nuts

Me: Sure. Mom left money for pizza anyway.

. . .

A GIF popped up on my screen of a person dancing in a full-blown flower costume. I rolled my eyes. She was such a weirdo.

Something banged from Parker's driveway, but instead of looking, like I wanted to, I walked out of my bedroom toward the shower. I congratulated myself on two things as the water warmed up. One, I held on to my plan to pretend Parker no longer existed. And two, I was finally taking the shower my mom had begged me to for days.

❧

"So." Madison held up two movies the second her bag hit the floor by the front door. "Funny love or sappy love?"

"And why couldn't we pick something on Netflix?" I reached for the red holders containing DVDs from Redbox. I didn't even know that thing still existed.

"We've seen all the good stuff."

I squinted at the titles. "I haven't even heard of these movies."

"Yeah, well, it was slim pickings." Madison snatched the disks from my hand. "We could always go out."

I gave a pointed look at my very flattering sweatpants and tattered tank top. She grinned and nudged her bag with her toe.

"I came prepared."

"Nope." I made my way to the kitchen, where a pint of Ben & Jerry's Half Baked awaited me. No way in hell was I playing dress up again. Last time that happened I ended up on the receiving end of a broken heart. Something I would prefer to avoid in the future.

"Okay, so I might not have been one-hundred-percent

honest. Billy McDermott is throwing a party tonight and I think we should go."

Didn't everyone get sick of parties? "How have you not learned from the last two? Parties and me don't end well."

"Except I know for a fact Parker won't be there. It's perfect. You get all hot and find yourself a new man to drool over."

"Or get dared into dating another one?"

Madison cringed from the anger in my statement as she sat down at the kitchen table.

At least she looked remorseful.

"I said I was sorry, like, a million times. I promised never to butt in again. What more do you want?"

"Dragging me to a party is butting in." I slammed the silverware drawer shut with my hip. "Parties suck and so do boys. I just want to get through this summer without another round of humiliation." I dug my spoon into the ice cream a little too aggressively. "Do you know what people are saying about me online?"

Okay, so I might have stalked a few classmates the night after the party. Twitter was the worst, with several very unflattering pictures of me trying not to cry and Madison screaming at Parker. Most of them were titled with #troubleinparadise and #caughtintheact. The latter was referring to Parker, but still painted me in a bad light. Blind idiot wasn't the look I was going for.

"I saw." Madison ran a finger over the worn wood of the kitchen table. "But screw them. They've already moved on to new things."

"So glad," I mumbled in the most sarcastic tone I could muster then shoved another heaping spoonful of ice cream in my mouth.

"So...no party?"

I gave Madison a look that said I would kill her if she brought it up again.

She threw her palms up in defeat. "Okay fine. But we're getting cheesy sticks with the pizza." She typed something into her phone, most likely telling Billy we couldn't make it. "If I'm staying in, I'm doing it right. And you're letting me borrow a pair of those ugly sweatpants." She looked up at me, eyebrow arched.

I grinned and tossed my spoon in the sink with a loud clatter. It was about time that Madison got a Lily make-under. "Sweatpants in the top drawer. I'll order pizza."

Madison did a little shimmy with a lot of boob jiggle as she stood up. "Five minutes. You better have ordered the pizza and picked a movie." She set her phone down on the kitchen counter where I left mine charging earlier. Knowing her, she would steal my charger the second she got back.

As her feet pounded up the stairs, I reached for my phone to call in the pizza. As it was ringing, I disconnected the charger and reached for Madison's phone. In the process of plugging it in, my finger hit the home button, lighting up the screen and revealing a text... from Parker.

"Thank you for calling MOD Pizza, can I place you on a quick hold?" The person on the other line spoke.

"S-sure." My ear filled with an audio recording of current offers and thanks for being patient. But I barely heard any of it. My hand shook as I stared down at his name. On my best friend's phone. A girl who three days prior had torn his head off for hurting me.

Several scenarios ran through my head. The most absurd being them hooking up behind my back. The most obvious explanation was Madison telling him off again via text. That still wasn't enough to quell the churning in my stomach. Telling him off or not, she shouldn't have texted him at all.

I heard a door open and shut followed by a few foot-steps and another door. Knowing Madison was in the bath-room, leaving me with only a few minutes to find out what the hell she was up to, I pressed the home button again and typed in her password when the phone prompted me.

Total best friend no-no, but so was texting an asshole who broke my heart.

With a lump in my throat, I clicked on their text exchange.

Parker: Thanks for trying.

It was the latest message, the one that displayed on the home screen. I scrolled up checking to see what prompted it.

Madison: Sorry I tried. If u want to make it up to her u better figure out something else.

I scrolled through their message exchange, most of which included Madison telling him off for hurting me, like a good best friend, and then Parker begging her to bring me to this party. None of it made any sense. Why would Madison go from angry to agreeing to bring me to a place she knew he would be at, when I made it clear I never wanted to see him again?

Madison walked into the room right as I had opened her call log and saw Parker's name plastered all over it. She gave me a confused look, matching my own, until she noticed the phone tucked against my shoulder and the other in my hand.

"Lily..." Her eyes went wide at the same time a person answered the line at the pizza joint.

I hung up on the pizza guy as fast as I could and tossed her phone at her. "You should go."

"I can explain." Madison fumbled with her phone, catching it before it fell to the tile floor.

"Explain why my best friend is chatting up the guy who tore out my heart and stomped on it?"

"Yes. I ripped his damn head off. You saw for yourself! I would never do anything that would hurt you."

"And the party?"

Madison's cheeks flushed red. "He begged me. He called and told me how sorry he was and that it was a misunderstanding. Tracy threw herself at him and he was trying to pry her off when we walked in. He wanted to make it up to you but knew you would avoid him."

"Yeah, sounds like a great excuse. Parker will say anything he can to get what he wants. And for whatever reason, he wants you to think he's a good guy so he can make my life miserable."

"Why do you think that is, huh?" Madison propped a hand on her hip changing from defensive to offensive.

"Because he's a dick?"

"Or maybe it's because he's crushing so hard, he doesn't know how to handle it. He's a guy—we both know they aren't too smart, especially when it comes to their emotions."

"Wow." I palmed my forehead and made a move toward

the door. "You can't be that stupid. He's playing with you and you're eating it up."

Madison blocked my path. She knew me well, and I was five seconds away from putting a locked bedroom door between us.

"Maybe you're the stupid one. Maybe he's been trying all week to tell you how he feels and every time he got close, you shut off like you always do! Just because your dad left doesn't mean every guy does."

The second the words were out, Madison's mouth popped open as if she couldn't believe what she said. I know I couldn't.

"You should go," I said between clenched teeth.

"Look, I'm sorry. You're right—it was over the line. But you should talk to him. You know I wouldn't push this if I thought for one second he was out to hurt you."

"Go."

"Lily, come on. You can't be pissed at a guy who you strung along all week. You played just as many games as he did, you're just too upset to realize it."

My heart fluttered at her words because as much as I hated to admit it, she was right. I was so back and forth every time my feelings surfaced that I probably gave both of us emotional whiplash. That aside, it still didn't excuse her from butting in.

"Please, just go."

Madison shoved her phone in her pocket and made her way to the living room. "Fine. Call me when you realize that I'm right." She slammed the door, shaking the painting that my mother did at one of those painting parties, that was hanging beside the door.

I glared at the door, hoping Madison could feel it through the cherrywood. The second I heard her car pull out of the driveway, I collapsed onto the sofa, four years of repressed tears streaming down my face. Not only had she betrayed me, she poured salt in my wound by bringing up my dad.

What a great best friend.

SEVENTEEN
Lily

My mom came home at half past ten and found me in a curled-up mess with our decorative blankets cocooning me.

A little after Madison left, I received a text from a number I no longer had stored in my phone. It was easy to guess who it was since it pleaded with me not be mad at Madison and that he coerced her into it.

So, my best friend ran to my former best friend and current heart-wrecker to tell him how much of a bitch I was being. Perfect. How else should an already craptastic day end?

Considering how much of a bad mood I had been in, my mom barely batted an eye. That was, until she saw my tear-streaked cheeks. Little known fact, my mom hadn't seen me cry since my dad left. I decided that day that no one would ever see that particular weakness again. Which is why she practically threw herself at me and pulled me into her lap.

To say that made my hysterics worse would be an understatement.

It took a while of her rocking and stroking my hair before I calmed down. See, I realized somewhere in my breakdown that the whole thing wasn't all due to Parker's maybe hook-up. That was crappy and hurt like hell, but I really had no right to be that mad. Not when he wasn't mine. All of my feelings just got muddled because the same year my dad held up an emotional middle finger to my family and bounced, so did Parker. And if I had to admit it, my tears were mostly about the lost friendship—twice—due to the emotional barbed wire I put up.

Like it or not, Madison was right. When it came to men, I was completely closed off. I could be as candid as the day was long with women, but the second I felt any connection with guys, I shut down. Same reason I shrugged off Milo leaving, because I never let myself fall for him. And he proved why when he left. Just like everyone else.

Halfway through this revelation I realized how melodramatic I sounded. I let four years of my life pass me by out of fear.

That made me cry more. Like a fricken floodgate burst and I couldn't close it.

When I ran out of extra water to leak out of my face, my mom kissed my temple and hugged me closer. "What happened, baby?"

"Do you want the short or long answer?" I wiped my nose on the blanket, vowing to wash it as soon as I got up, and moved so I could look her in the eye.

"Long, of course." My mom tucked me under her arm, resting her chin on my head.

"Parker and I stopped being friends in eighth grade."

She let out a little chuckle that she covered with another kiss on my hair. "I know that, sweetie. I kinda noticed when my grocery bill went down, and you stopped having so many dare-induced injuries."

Dares. The same thing that brought me to the point of repressed tears. They held a long tradition in Parker's and my friendship, which is how I ended up with the jagged scar under my lip. Neither one of us was fond of turning them down.

"Well, I have a new one, but I don't think the doctor can fix a broken heart."

"What happened?"

I sighed and twisted a loose strand on the blanket between my fingers. "The first day of break, Madison and I went to a party. We got roped into a game of truth or dare, and I was dared to date Parker for the summer."

"So that's why he was hanging around more often?"

"Uh-huh. And the only reason he invited me to the lake house."

"Okay... So how does this end with a broken heart? You and Parker drifted apart years ago."

"We drifted apart because he pushed me away. I've been in love with him since I was old enough to love boys, and he threw it back in my face. *Twice*." The admission physically hurt. My mom and I were close, but not that close. I kept my private life private when it came to her.

She leaned to the side, laying her hands on my shoulders so she could stare at me head-on. "Explain."

"Everything seemed like it was getting back to normal at the lake house, you know? We joked, we messed around, we flirted..." I went ahead and left the kiss out. I didn't want my mom to have a stroke from shock or elation. "And then I found him kissing a girl from school."

"Which is the real reason you came home early," she guessed correctly.

"Right."

"Did you and Madison do that thing where you ran out and didn't let him talk?"

Damn, my mom was good.

"Maybe."

"Sweetie..." She brushed hair out of my face, cupping my cheek in her favorite mom move. "I'm going to say something that might make you mad."

I tensed. Madison I could take—kind of—having my mom call me out on my faults might shatter me.

"You can't assume that everyone is like your father. He couldn't hang, and I know that's a crappy thing to do, but to be honest, we don't need him. I think I've done a bang-up job myself, and I would hope you agree. But not everyone is your dad. Most guys aren't, actually. Parker has been in love with you for as long as I can remember. You might not have seen it, but I did."

"You're only saying that because you're my mom and trying to make me feel better."

"No, I'm telling you the truth. I figured you both would come to this conclusion on your own, but apparently you're both too stubborn when it comes to your feelings." She sighed, patting my knee in an almost condescending way. "I can say with utmost certainty that he is in love with you. No boy, I don't care who they are, would go to the lengths he has gone for you if they weren't."

"What the hell are you talking about?"

She ignored my tone, a first for her. We may be close, but she still had rules. Disrespect was a big one.

"Oh, I don't know... How about the fact that he checked in with me regularly when you were dating Milo, offering to beat the crap out of him if he hurt you? Or how about the summer you had your wisdom teeth out, and he went to the store and got you all your favorite soft foods and made me promise not to tell you it was from him."

My wisdom teeth were extracted the summer between freshman and sophomore year. Parker was just a blip on my radar. In fact, most of that year he seemed a little less annoying than usual.

"I could go on and on and, believe me when I tell you, he asked about you every time he saw me. He wanted to know about your life, and I have a feeling it was because he regretted that he was no longer in it. You both had crappy things happen to you and you both dealt with it in different ways. You can't fault him for that."

"He left me when I needed him."

"And you pushed him away the second he showed any kind of weakness. He needed some space and instead you cut him out."

Damn.

Just like I had realized earlier. I had built up a wall so thick that when Parker tried to talk to me halfway through eighth grade, I blew him off. After all, I already had Madison.

"Talk to him." She patted my knee and got up. "Then I expect a big, fancy, mom-daughter dinner when you find out that I was right." She kissed my head then went upstairs.

I sat staring at my phone where it rested in my lap. Too much had happened in the course of a few days, and I was fairly certain my head was about to explode. But a part of me wanted to hear his side of the story, from him. He may have been able to spew things to Madison over the phone and have her believe him, but if I looked in his eyes when he was telling me, I would know for sure if he was lying.

With a shaky breath, I responded to his text.

Me: Can we talk...tomorrow?

· · ·

His response was instantaneous.

Parker: Yes please. Meet me at my house at noon? I have something I want to show u.

Interesting... His text made me want to run over there right then, but my face was that of horror movies after crying. Seriously, it might have been the reason I decided crying wasn't my thing and held everything inside instead.

Me: Noon it is. And Parker...I'm sorry.

With that, I switched my phone off, something I rarely did because I liked being connected. I heard the shower running, so I decided to get a jump start on beauty sleep. If I woke up early enough, there was a chance I would be able to work some voodoo magic and hide the puffy eyes I would be saddled with.

EIGHTEEN
Parker

LILY: ...I'm sorry.

I stared at those words for hours as I lay in bed. I couldn't quite figure out what she was sorry for. After all, I was the one who paraded Tracy around the party and got caught in a compromising position. If I had kept my head on straight like Hunter told me to do, the night might have ended differently.

With me telling her I was out-of-the-world in love with her.

Well past midnight, I set my phone on the nightstand and tried to sleep. It was no use. Around and around, my thoughts chased each other. Both possible reactions from Lily. The good and the heartbreaking. I kept wanting to walk over there and drag her out of the house to show her what I spent the day building for her when I should have been at swimming practice.

It was a conversation I would need to have with my dad after I sorted everything out with Lily. I hoped I would be in a better mood, because I would need it to face off with my dad about swimming. And maybe if I had Lily by my side, I could draw strength from her.

Then again, my whole plan was riding on Lily hearing me out. Past experiences showed that when upset, she wasn't good at listening.

Dragging her best friend into the mess only made things worse. I might have had a better shot without her, but at the time, I was desperate. Especially after I caught her peeking at me from inside her house and then refusing to come out. Again, from past experience, I figured she would spend the whole summer avoiding me, and wouldn't even think about hearing me out long enough to get her to my house.

With a sigh, I threw my arm over my eyes to block out the moonlight flowing through the gap in the drapes I forgot to close. Okay, maybe not forgot, more along the line of left open hoping I would catch a glimpse of Lily because I was that desperate. Unfortunately, her blinds remained closed tight.

Not even twelve hours to go. Twelve hours separated me from either heartbreak or happiness. Knowing I wouldn't be able to sleep, I got up and threw on my jeans and a hoodie with the plan of taking a drive to clear my head. My dad passed out early after a couple of glasses of scotch, so it wasn't as if he would notice.

I grabbed my keys from the hook next to the door then slipped out as quietly as possible. I had gotten good at it over the years, so really, I had no reason to be jumpy. That was, until I bumped into a body on my porch.

No joke, I almost screamed. Almost.

Lily jumped back, her hand flying to her heart as I gripped my stomach and tried to breathe.

"You scared the crap out of me!" Lily whisper-yelled, her heightened anxiety making her voice come out higher than normal.

"I scared you? You're the one skulking around my porch."

She glanced away, but even in the yellow glow from my porch light, I could see her cheeks turn pink.

"Yeah...well... I kind of couldn't wait to talk to you, but then I changed my mind. I changed my mind about ten times since I've been standing out here, actually."

Her words gave me hope. A ray of sunshine cutting through the cloudiness in my heart. I reached for her hand, surprised when she didn't pull away, and tugged her down the steps toward the gate that led to my backyard. "I want to show you something."

"Now?" she asked but didn't put up a fight.

Yes. Now.

She was there, and the second I saw her face I knew I couldn't wait until morning. Especially when I noticed how puffy her eyes were. They looked like that the day after my mom died. I knew she had been crying and if it was because of me, which I had a hunch it was, I wanted to take those bad feelings away.

I reached over the top of the fence and undid the latch, thankful that my dad's room faced the other way.

"Close your eyes." I stopped before we turned the corner and my surprise came into view.

"Is this where you murder me? 'Cause it kind of feels like that type of moment."

"Please," I snorted. "If I wanted to murder you, I had plenty of time at the lake house. A perfect place to dump the body too like that one creepy movie where the guy has a garden of dead women under the lake."

"*Cabin by the Lake!*" Lily smacked my arm and giggled. "I always knew you connected with that character too much."

"You caught me." I smiled and covered her eyes with my hand. "Now close 'em and keep 'em closed till I tell you."

"Exactly what a killer would say." She laughed but did as I said, her eyelashes tickling my palm as her eyes closed.

With a stomach full of what had to be raging wasps, I led her to the middle of my backyard where I had sweated all day building an amazing replica of the tree house we had as kids. Except this time, I built it on the ground.

"Okay, open them." I let her go and stepped to the side.

Lily did as I said. It took her a moment, but I knew the exact second she noticed it, because her breath caught in her throat and her hand reached out to grip my arm.

"Parker... Is this our old fort?"

"As close as I could get it. Had to put it on the ground since Dad ripped down our tree."

Her eyes found mine, wide with what I hoped was excitement, because I sure as hell was excited.

"Why?"

"Come here, let me show you."

She took my hand as I led her up to the small entrance. I tried to make the walls higher, but we still had to duck to get through the front door.

I switched on the camping lantern I had taken from the garage and watched carefully as Lily took in the decorations I covered the walls with. Finding those photos had come in handy after all and it was worth it to see the look on her face.

"Parker..."

"Lily." I squeezed her hand, trying to ignore the shaking in mine. "I'm terrible with how I feel. It used to take my mom pointing it out before I even understood it. That was true with everything. Swimming. Writing. You..." Her eyes met mine, and I swallowed hard not knowing if I should continue.

"Me?"

"Yeah, Lily, you. See, my mom picked up on it first. The day you busted your face on that hill, I was out of my mind with worry. When they didn't let me go to the hospital with you to get your stitches, I locked myself in my room and refused to come out until you got back."

"Later that night my mom pulled me aside and asked me what made me so scared. The fact that you were hurt or the fact that you wouldn't talk to me about it? It was that moment I realized losing you would be like taking all the color out of the world. And I loved color."

Lily's breath picked up and she squeezed my hand so hard I thought it might break. But I didn't shy away. A broken bone would be a hell of a lot better than a broken heart.

"It was a secret I kept to myself for a while... For seven years." I grinned, trying to ease some of the tension, but Lily didn't move. Didn't blink. "My plan was to tell you at Christmas the year we turned thirteen. It was your favorite holiday, and I thought maybe I could make it mine too if you felt the same way. Only problem was, my mom died that summer. Suddenly the color really was gone from my world. Light too. It left me in such a dark place that I didn't want to drag you down with me. I wanted to preserve your light."

Lily stepped closer, her free hand trailing up my arm until it rested on my shoulder.

"My mom always knew about how I felt, and suddenly I didn't have anyone in my corner. No one to root for us or tell me how to feel. I shut down right when you needed me most and when I finally came to my senses, we were over.

You had Madison and Milo and I figured I did it to myself so I would have to live with it. Problem was, every day felt like walking through mud and when I would see you in the halls that mud, became a little easier to tread. But you refused to acknowledge me so I went about getting your attention in the only way I knew how. You always were a hothead."

Laughing, Lily brought her face closer to mine. I wanted to wrap her up in a tight hug and kiss the breath right out of her, but I needed to finish. Four years of unrequited love couldn't be silenced.

"What happened at the lake wasn't what you thought. My plan was to spend that week fixing all the damage four years and a crap-ton of resentment caused. But every time we came close, one of us would shut down. See, the thing I never thought of was how wrecked our hearts were. And what you walked in on would never have happened if I didn't throw Tracy in your face in a last-ditch effort to get your attention. Nothing happened, you need to know that. I need you to know—"

Lily's lips crashed into mine, taking me by surprise. I took a staggered step backward, about all the room the tiny space would allow, before my spine pressed into the wall. Lily's hands were in my hair in an instant, her body flush against my chest as she dominated my mouth in a way I had never experienced.

Her tongue ran laps around mine, as if she needed to get it all out before something ruined it. Before we ruined it.

Not a chance of that happening this time.

I broke away from her with a gentle shove. There was nothing I wanted more than to continue, but I needed to get one last thing out.

"Lily, I love you. I've loved you since the day you took

my dare and raced down that hill even though you knew it would end badly. I might be terrible at expressing myself, so I built you this fort and filled it with photographic evidence of our love. Platonic and not."

I tapped a photo of us at twelve, both dressed up for our first official school dance.

Her eyes took in the picture as a smile spread across her beautiful lips. "I almost kissed you that night. But you ran off with Marco Flores to TP Principal Beck's car."

"Guess I need to make up for that." I threaded my hands into her hair, bringing her face to mine. She placed a gentle peck on my lips before leaning back.

"In case you were wondering, Hayes... I love you too."

My heart glowed in my chest. A lightness I hadn't felt since my mom was alive. Those three words were all I ever wanted to hear from her mouth.

"Truth or dare?"

Lily bit her lip in an effort to keep the grin off her face. "Dare."

"I dare you to spend the rest of your life being honest with your feelings and not letting the crappy shit in our past scare you off."

She pretended to think about it before bringing her mouth to mine again. "Only if you're right by my side," she whispered against my lips.

I couldn't think of one good reason why not. So I answered with a kiss.

EPILOGUE
Lily

"Okay, smile." My mom held up her phone and snapped a photo of Parker and me next to his car. Apparently once word got out that we were officially a thing, my mom took that to mean documenting every single day.

"We're going to be late." I covered my face as she tried to take another photo. Parker, being no help at all, cheesed it up at my side with an arm draped over my shoulders.

"Okay. Okay." She dropped her phone long enough that I left my defenses down. And...that's when she snapped another photo.

I'm sure I looked charming. Couldn't wait to see what kind of expression that picture caught.

"Bye, Mom!" I yelled as I climbed into the car.

"Have a great first day!" She gave me an over-the-top wave before she went back inside. I was positive the neighbors must think she was crazy.

"Think your mom will ever get over the fact that we're together?" Parker asked as he started the engine.

"Highly doubtful. Like I said, it's her dream come true."

"My mom, too." Parker grabbed my hand, entwining our fingers as he drove away from the curb.

"Senior year," I sighed. "How's that going to feel without swimming?"

He grimaced and bobbed one shoulder. Over the summer he'd sat down and talked to his dad about quitting the swim team. To say his father had a coronary would be an understatement. I sat with Parker the whole time as his dad yelled until he ran out of steam. When Parker finally admitted that swimming reminded him too much of his mom, Mr. Hayes gave in.

They came to the agreement that his dad would rent out the lake house when we weren't up there. It would help pay for college, but Parker still needed a job to offset the costs. Luckily for me, we both scored jobs at the mall. Food court dates had gotten a little stale, but as long as I was with him, it didn't matter too much.

We pulled into the senior parking lot, and right away, I spotted Madison with a very smug-looking Aiden wrapped around her. It was disgusting, but all my fault so I couldn't complain.

True to my word, I set them up. All it took was a surprise blind date to make her realize how crazy she was about him. And they had been inseparable ever since. One giant pile of PDA that on most days made me want to gag. Parker and I were a little more low-key.

I didn't want anyone getting ideas about how amazing my boyfriend was. And the things that boy could do to my body with a single kiss would make the female population weak in the knees just by witnessing it.

"It's the Maiden Monster," Parker joked, as he parked in the spot next to my flushed best friend.

"I'm surprised they are out in the daylight."

Parker flashed me his grin that I came to realize wasn't so cocky after all, as he climbed out of the car.

"Eww, break it up." I hip-checked Madison as I closed my door. "Young children around. We don't want to frighten them."

"We're in the senior parking lot," Madison said between kisses. "Besides, can't be worse than the show Parker put on at the bonfire."

Ouch. Sore subject. But I brushed it away. We couldn't spend our lives looking to the past. It had a way of hindering the present.

Parker slung his arm around my shoulders. "Should I get the hose?" he whispered in my ear.

"Only if it's attached to a fire truck. Pretty sure that's what we'll need to break them apart."

Aiden groaned and pulled away to send a dirty look in my direction. "We can hear you."

"That was the point, genius."

"Buy me a cookie?" Madison pouted with her hands knotted in Aiden's shirt.

"My cookie wants a cookie? You got it." He turned around so she could launch off the back of his truck onto his back.

"Are we that gross?" I asked Parker.

"Yes!" Maiden answered, then broke into simultaneous giggles.

So gross.

"Come on, cookie," Parker mocked, in the most obnoxious lovey-dovey voice he could muster as he led me toward the front entrance.

Senior year.

I gazed up at the building in a new way. When I entered high school, my heart was still raw from the loss of Parker. Walking in on my last first day ever as a high school student with Parker right next to me, I couldn't keep my heart rate down or the smile from my face.

In a very short period, we would be adults. The following year, Parker and I planned on attending the same college. With a scholarship out of the picture, he had to settle on a different path, one that didn't include an out-of-state college. I always dreamed of going to UDUB and with it close to home we would be able to save money. He said he didn't care, as long as he was with me. He was still undecided on what he wanted to major in, so to him, the campus we attended didn't make much of a difference.

Never in a million years did I think a stupid dare at an even stupider high school party would lead me back to the boy I loved and lost so many years before.

I guess, sometimes, you just need to take the long route. In the end, you might appreciate it a hell of a lot more. Scars and all.

A.R. Perry is an American-born author who has lived all over the US due to her wanderlust husband. She has a degree in photography and massage therapy yet somehow works in human resources.

When she's not working, reading, or writing she can be found sleeping because the day is practically done. Thank goodness for coffee, chocolate, and Panic! At The Disco or nothing would ever get done.

Lost Atlantic
DESIGNS

Made in the USA
Coppell, TX
02 December 2021

66869348R00111